GRAVE GIRL

THE ACCIDENTAL REAPER PARANORMAL URBAN FANTASY SERIES, BOOK 4

MISTY EVANS

Beach Path Publishing

ONE

"A witch, a vampire, and a shifter walk into a bar..." Andy scanned the room before us. Music blared, patrons yelled and laughed, and I stifled the urge to run. We were between the Super Bowl and Mardi Gras, Valentine's Day only a few days away, but this place didn't offer a whiff of any of those mundane celebrations. It was hardcore supernatural.

His girlfriend, Aurora, pinched his arm. "Focus."

The wolf shifter jerked. "You haven't even heard the rest of the joke."

"Why is there no grim in it?" I asked.

He winked good-naturedly. "I was getting to that."

Killion, the master vampire in our entourage, zeroed in on two men in a booth nearby. Their heads were together in what appeared to be a conspiring conversation. "We are surrounded by powerful creatures, none of whom will take well to our presence if we step on toes. This is a reconnaissance mission. If we locate the Fae princess, Aurora will befriend her." He glanced at the witch, who was posing as one of the beings I hadn't known existed until a few weeks ago. "If all goes well, and the opportunity presents itself, draw her outside and Chloe and I shall handle it from there, but don't push. If you arouse her suspicions, she'll disappear on us."

Aurora nodded. For tonight's operation, part of an ongoing investigation for Soul Management Group, she'd transformed herself into a blonde with slightly pointed ears and vivid blue eyes. "Don't worry. I'll get her to the alley."

Those irises, more than the change in hair color, kept tripping me up. She often transfigured into a panther with those same peepers, and I kept waiting for the rest of her to morph. "Don't take any unnecessary chances," I warned. "Princess Harmony seems like a Disney faery with her petite frame and innocent charm, but she's Grimm Brothers-level dangerous. She'll giggle one moment and rip out your throat the next."

Andy leaned close to the witch, his long reddish hair brushing her shoulder as he spoke in her ear, too low for me, even with my enhanced grim hearing—aided by Killion's vampire blood—to catch. I saw her expression soften. She cupped his face in her hand and nodded. After a lengthy gaze into each other's eyes that denoted a mental conversation, they broke apart and he spoke to Killion and me. His nose twitched as if it itched. "She's definitely here. I scent the hallmarks of her kind."

Four months ago, I was a normal twenty-four-year-old attending college and working two jobs in Danté's Grove, Louisiana. After being attacked by a grim reaper and killing him, I was plunged into the world of death and the supernatural. I was introduced to the things of nightmares and this bar was full of them.

Vampires, shapeshifters, powerful witches, and evil wizards—I'd encountered all types. My boss was Death. You'd think by now, nothing would surprise me, but learning that the Fae, along with pixies, trolls, and elves existed honestly shocked the reaper robes right off me.

I sniffed the air, but all I could strongly detect above the other odors was dog, thanks to my psychopomp, Ghost, who liked to sleep on my robes. The *eau de bar* was laced with stale beer and greasy wings. The only other notable aroma was Killion's warm caramel and old libraries scent. It was all over me, since we'd come directly from the warmth of his bed when Aurora had called with the news that Harmony Fairweather had tripped one of her magical alerts and was in the area.

I hadn't had time to shower, and I kinda didn't care. The master vampire and I had recently begun a romantic relationship that still had me reeling from the intensity of it. I was head over heels for the guy.

I *did* regret not eating before we'd hustled out of the penthouse to join Andy and Aurora, but apprehending Harmony should be quick and easy, once we had her in the alley. The trick was getting her there. "I don't see her." I scanned the place again. "What I do see is a lot of magical residue and far too many ghosts."

"Your grave sight is growing stronger." Killion touched my low back, the corner of his mouth quirking with smug satisfaction. "Told you it would."

I tried not to roll my eyes. We'd shared each other's blood, and when we'd become intimate, not only had he resurrected my dead love life—and thank all that was holy for that—he'd told me my natural abilities would increase exponentially because of the sexual energy we shared. It heightened everything.

So while I was no shifter like Andy, nor vampire as was Killion, I could sense and spot the glow of magic and interact with earthbound souls as easily as I could those still living. In fact, I walked between the worlds of life and death, and at times, I couldn't tell the difference between those who were corporeal and those who weren't.

A pulse of magic rippled over my skin and raised gooseflesh. It reminded me of the feel of stardust I'd experienced a few months ago when Death had almost killed me on a trip through the cosmos. I'd earned a white streak in my hair that I preferred to dye the same violet as Killion's eyes. Unfortunately, I'd let it go too long and it was silvery once more.

"She smells like elderberry wine," Andy said. His voice was tinged with yearning.

Aurora sounded dreamy and far away when she added, "And summer days in the forest."

"Moonlight kisses." Killion's voice was a purr and the sound made certain parts of my anatomy tingle.

"Wow." I glanced at them. Pure bliss shone on their faces. Had that pulse done this? More importantly, why was I immune? I snapped my fingers in their collective faces. "Grim to Scooby Gang. What's wrong with you guys? Maybe I better handle this myself."

Each blinked as if waking from a dream. "I'm fine," Aurora said.

Andy tugged at the crotch of his pants. "I'm not. That's some powerful mojo she's slinging around."

Killion frowned and edged closer to me. "She's using her charm magic to test everyone who walks into the place."

"Why?" I asked.

"To see if we're prey."

I scanned the bar again. Harmony Fairweather, Fae princess or not, was going down.

TWO

"No one is going to end up her prey tonight," I announced. "She's done, once and for all." Due to Killion's push, the two conspirators from the booth stumbled drunkenly to the door, freeing up a seat for us. Several patrons had noticed us and were watching. We needed to blend in. "Sit."

Aurora cast her attention about. "But—"

I pointed to the bench, sticky from things I didn't want to think about. "Chill, faery girl. You'll have your chance in a minute. If she's using magic to turn you all into lust zombies, we better reinforce our plan."

"I don't know what came over me," Killion said. He zoomed in on a table of shifters pinning him and Andy with curious looks. They hurriedly glanced away.

"What's up with them?" I cocked my chin in their direction.

"Nothing of importance." His tone told me he was stopping trouble before it had a chance to start. "We need to dull our olfactory senses."

Andy sniffed the air and his lids fluttered. "How do we do that?"

"I can use a charm," Aurora volunteered. "It will wear off in an hour, but that should give us enough time to lure her into our trap, right?"

Killion considered it. Vampires and witches tended to distrust each other, but honestly, few in the supernatural community liked the Undead. "If that's the best option, fine."

Apparently it wasn't. I nudged him. "Do you have an alternative?"

"I cannot switch off my sense of smell any more than I can stop being half-vampire."

My faery-looking friend grinned, a glint of mischief in her eyes. "Will I be the first witch to bespell the great Killion Reveux?"

He flashed his fangs and the pulse of magic he sent her way made my bones shudder. "You may discover it is not something to brag about."

Her grin widened. *Thin ice,* I mentally thought at her. Ignoring my warning, she made a motion as if she were checking an invisible box. "Bucket list item one hundred forty two, done."

Killion growled and Andy growled back. My hand went under the table to rest on Killion's thigh before he made use of his fangs. "Cool it, all of you. One minute you're high on lust, and now you're goading each other into a fight."

Killion's gaze slid away and Aurora shook herself. "Sorry," she said. "This Fae magic is so..." She visibly shivered.

"Primal," Killion finished. There was an edge to his voice that made my already tense body hum with protectiveness. "More so than I anticipated. She is royalty. The High Fae possess magic equal to ours, just...distinct."

Great. "You're sure the magic suppressing belt that Death gave me will work on her, right?" It was my only hope of taking her alive so SMG could interrogate her about the husks of three human victims Killion and I had discovered in the abandoned Longgrove Arboretum ten miles north of town.

They'd been sucked dry—there was no other way to describe it. Their shells had been papery, their bones turning to dust if we so much as breathed on them. What kind of supernatural could do that? The best guess SMG had was the ancient and elusive Fae.

The princess had made a spectacle of herself, going against Fae decorum and norms. She'd been anything but subtle and had made her proclivities for human and supernatural partners alike well known. Her hunting ground was the bar and grill.

Fae embraced the elements and seasons. Her element was air and she was from the Autumn Court. That alone wasn't enough to throw suspicion on her, but the fact she'd set up her own "court" here at Tipsy's, and eyewitnesses placed our victims in the place over the past three weeks, did.

"I have backup, just in case," Aurora said, patting her bag. "I already used it to disguise my witch scent, but it should work for this, too."

"I'm the backup." Killion didn't seem excited about

the prospect. "I would, nonetheless, find your potion to diminish her enticing aroma helpful."

Enticing? My hackles rose. I had the urge to claim him right there in the bar for all to see.

Down girl. I forced myself to relax.

He'd once told me my scent was unique. It was one of the things that had attracted him to me. No one else running around in the world was Grim Zero—only me. At the beginning of time, I'd been the one and only reaper created, my job had been to protect Death. A lot had happened since then, but that's why Killion craved my blood, and the richness of its essence was its own kind of aphrodisiac. "Maybe we should rethink this. I'd prefer my *backup* wasn't attracted to my quarry."

He tugged on my braid, shorter than it had been after I'd cut it, but I'd discovered my magic caused my hair to grow quickly and it was long once more. His heated, roguish grin made my toes curl. "Jealous, are you?"

The attraction between us was still new, vulnerable. Our bond was unbreakable, eternal, yet there were times when it left me blindsided with its intensity and my reaction to that.

Grabbing him by the back of the neck, I brought my lips to his. The kiss was hot, possessive, and my own magic flooded the bar. When I broke away, we were both panting and all eyes were on us. The raucous talking and laughing had come to a halt.

"Well," he said, brushing a thumb over my bottom lip. "You have nothing to worry about. My desire for you is all-consuming."

Andy watched with interest; Aurora looked away, cheeks heating.

"Don't forget it, Fang Boy." I nipped him with my teeth. "You're mine."

He inclined his head, a subservient gesture, and the whole bar sucked in a collective breath. A master vampire bowing to anyone was unheard of. "And you are mine, Grim."

"Now that we have that settled." Aurora rummaged in the tiny bag, which didn't look big enough to hold more than a tube of gloss. What she withdrew did indeed resemble a roll-on lip balm. "Hold out your palms."

Killion snarled at the onlookers and they all hastily returned to their drinking and carousing. He and Andy did as instructed while she uncapped the tube. She used the tip to draw a symbol in each of their palms, then hers. "Now rub your hands together."

Killion screwed up his nose. "That's disgusting."

Over the stale beer, fried food tang, and underlaying fragrances of various supernaturals, the potion's odor wafted around us. Dead locust, licorice, and wet clay mixed together in a revolting perfume.

Familiar with her wacky combos of ingredients for spells and potions that reeked and tasted awful, I grinned. "The worse the smell, the more effective the magic." It was one of her favorite responses when I groused about the teas she made me drink for various purposes, like suppressing my Grim Zero alter ego. Thank goodness I didn't need this lovely brew. "Now you understand why I complain about drinking my necro medicine and I'm entirely thrilled that I can't smell our lovely killer."

Aurora stuck her tongue out. "You're incorrigible."

"Good thing you love me."

As they rubbed it into their hands, I felt a tug in my diaphragm toward the closed banquet room doors. No one had come in or out, but the presence of someone very earthy and yet not of this world seeped out through them. My stomach cramped and I sucked in a breath. "Heads up," I uttered quietly. A dozen thoughts and images rode the wave of energy, sliding under my skin. "She's aware we're here and is about to make an appearance."

"Pretty sure everyone in the county knows we're here after that kiss," Andy said.

Killion's eyes followed mine. "You sense her?"

"Don't you?"

A crease appeared between his brows. He sniffed the air. "I do not. It seems the potion has done more than squelch my olfactory sense."

That *was* powerful. Aurora scratched at the tattoo on her wrist. It glowed a lime green color. "It's reacting oddly to her magic. I don't know why."

The tug inside me nearly brought me to my feet. A dead houseplant in a macramé holder near the window suddenly revived and began growing luscious leaves. "Oh no," I said, right before the doors opened.

But it wasn't the princess whose gold eyes locked on mine. From across the expanse, a huge male filled the opening. His silver hair was pulled back from his face, several sections braided and secured at the nape of his neck. A tattoo that marked him as royalty swirled down the side of his neck and disappeared into his wine colored tunic with a golden sun embroidered on the left breast. Along with it, he wore black slacks and leather boots.

A twig of variegated ivy twined in one silver braid, and as I held his gaze—because I couldn't look away—it came alive like the plant and circled down onto his shoulder.

The Fae male arched a brow at me and his lips twitched, amused.

Killion was always cool and detached, his vampire nature preternaturally still. At the focused attention on me, he became even more so, signaling what I'd learned to be tightly-coiled rage. He was a weapon under his designer suits and modern accruements, and after bonding with me, he was my ultimate protector.

As master vampire, he reigned supreme in Danté's Grove; as my lover, he did so in my heart. The territorial nature of his actions toward me could be a tad over the top, yet to him, they were perfectly natural. Any male, supernatural or not, who got too close or showed the slightest bit of sexual interest in me, brought out his dominate alpha male.

At that moment, he exuded enough *I'm going to kill you vibes*, the whole bar fell deathly silent once more.

THREE

I touched his thigh under the table once more, refusing to look away and break eye contact with the Fae male.

While Killion's protective and territorial reaction was appreciated, I knew the Laws of Nature and the Elemental Kingdom. To look away first was to submit, and I wasn't good at that. "Easy," I murmured, knowing full well the pointed ears of the creature in the doorway picked up my words. "We didn't come to start a fight." I hoped both males got the point. *No trouble.* "We're here to enjoy ourselves," I lied. "That's all."

A petite female sashayed past the ogling Fae, swinging in front of him, laughing. Long tresses, big blue eyes, and the most perfect skin I'd ever seen. Lithe and curvy, she grabbed his hand and used him like a maypole, causing him to break eye contact. "Where is my drink, Prince Ozmeus?" She trailed her fingers over his massive chest and shoulder. "The king take you for making me wait."

Two female companions appeared behind her, one a smiling faery with equally generous curves, the other human and looking slightly dazed. The silver-haired male gently detached her grip. "Return to the room and I will bring it shortly, your majesty."

She glanced in our direction, and although we were across the room, I heard every word. "The vampire is no threat, are you?" She winked at Killion and my hand on his leg tightened.

Against her bodyguard's wishes, she skipped to our table. The place remained quiet as a graveyard. Even the barkeep had turned off the TV broadcasting a basketball game, and the jukebox had stopped mid-song.

Although she appeared drunk and harmless, the clarity in her eyes suggested anything but. "You're *gorgeous.*" She leaned on the table, making heavy eye contact with Killion. "Do you possess Fae blood? I've never seen any with violet eyes who didn't."

My own territorial instincts went nuclear. "Mine." The single word came out low and menacing, my lip curling.

My companions gaped. It was Killion's turn to hold me back. I wanted to rip her limb from limb.

The prince was instantly at her side, a calming smile on his face as he loomed over her. He generated enough heat to make me instantly roast. "I believe he is spoken for," he said to her, then to us added, "Please excuse my cousin. She is recovering from a broken heart and is unfamiliar with the mores of your kingdom."

"Of course," Aurora said with a bright smile. At the

same time she kicked me under the table. "Perhaps you'd like to join us."

"Ouch," I yelped, rubbing my shin. I shot her a glare and kicked her back, satisfied when she flinched. "In what kingdom is it okay to poach someone's boyfriend?"

Killion's fingers tightened around mine. "I'm sure she didn't realize our connection."

Total lie. We'd "marked" each other, as the supernatural community termed it, with our exclusive bond, and everyone could sense the fact we'd shared blood. It was no light matter. Not a fling or a casual dating situation. A mated pairing was stronger than a blood contract, and it ran deeper than any human marriage vow or legal paper.

I'd never expected to be in such an unbreakable, if totally amazing, relationship. My bond with him drove my thoughts, words, and actions.

And right now, I wanted to kill the princess who still stared at him with enough lust in her eyes to make me see red.

She gave an abashed bat of her long lashes. "You should be more careful making deals."

The Fae were known for manipulating humans, as well as many in the supernatural community, with carefully worded bargains and covert contracts that appeared as nothing but simple conversation. Aurora had warned me not to answer any questions they might pose, or offer any help. I could find myself bound to one of them, regardless of my power and status.

Another wave of trippy magic burst around us, making the spot between my legs throb. Other patrons felt it, too. All manner of kissing, clothing removal, and undulating bodies began. Those with more control slipped out the door, seeking privacy.

The master vampire didn't so much as blink. A good thing, since I was becoming angrier by the second. His hand gripped me tight, whether to stop me from reaping her or himself from causing a fight, I wasn't sure. The previous coiled tension returned and he sent out his own magic, forming a shield. "And you should refrain from preying on those in my territory."

The cat was out of the bag now. Harmony's eyes glittered. "Prey?" She gestured to the two females with her. The human had fallen into the other's arms and was kissing her madly. All around us, the bar had erupted in an orgy. "She came to me willingly, as do all who spend time with me. I have no need to *hunt* for friends or lovers, unlike—"

Ozmeus touched her elbow. "Princess, tonight is for revelry, not arguments." A sudden calm stole over her. "Let's get you that drink."

He motioned at her friends and they broke apart to link an arm with hers, guiding her toward the bar. The barkeep watched with fascination. She didn't even glance back at us, but was soon pawing at one of her companions while the orgy continued.

This was not at all how I'd expected the night to go.

Ozmeus placed a business card onto the table. "Once more, I ask your forgiveness. She is harmless, if misguided. We seek fun and freedom from the constraints of our realm, and we want no trouble with you or your friends. In fact, if you should find yourself in need of assistance, I offer you my services." He tapped the card and slid it toward me, even as he held Killion's gaze. "One favor at the time of your choosing, as long as it does not violate the laws of me and mine."

Aurora sucked in a breath, eyes wide. She started to reach for it, as if needing to touch it. Touch *him*. I knocked her hand away before she could. "Why?" I asked.

He kept his focus pinned on the vampire. "Your friends are causing us problems and I wish it to stop. Consider this a contribution to that end."

I frowned. Was he trying to bribe us?

Andy reared back. "We haven't done anything."

Killion's face remained impassive, yet his grip suggested he was still on high alert. "Which friends?"

The prince pointed out the dirty window, the hanging plant still working long tendrils toward me. "The Undead."

A black tour bus had rolled into the lot, taking up a dozen spaces. The windows were tinted, and a pair of red lips with fangs and dripping blood was custom painted on the side.

As we leaned closer to the glass and I brushed the green plant out of the way, the door opened and a male with blond spiked hair, cheekbones that could cut glass, and metal piercings all over his visible skin, disembarked. A woman in flowing lace and hooker heels trailed out after him, and more vampires followed, joking and laughing as they crossed the lot toward the building.

In one fluid movement, Killion came to his feet and yanked me out of the booth. The wave of magic the visitors sent out stopped all activity around us and a handful of patrons frantically snatched up discarded clothes, nearly trampling each other running for the back exit. "Go. Now," Killion said. "The penthouse. Stay there until I come for you."

"But—"

He pushed me toward the rear of the bar. "Do it," he snarled.

My blood vibrated with the command. Andy and Aurora took my arms and hustled me past Ozmeus, just as the spikey-haired vampire came through the front door. "Killion," I heard him say in a melodic tone. "It's been too long." And then he added, "*Brother.*"

FOUR

"I'm not leaving him." I yanked away from Andy and Aurora's grips. The alley was lit by a single light on top of a pole, spotlighting the patrons who'd fled scattering into the shadowy night. "Who are those vampires? Did that guy say 'brother'?"

Moss appeared at the end of the alley, a linebacker-sized member of Killion's nest who chauffeured his master. He lumbered toward me. "We leave now."

"Why?" I was shaking from head to toe. "Is he in danger?"

"Not him," a familiar Fae voice said. Ozmeus stood in the exit. "You. Go, so he does not need to worry about your safety. I will stand by his side if he needs reinforcements."

Moss glared at the male. "My family is on the way."

"And I have no doubt he can hold his own," the prince said with a smile. The rotten garbage odor morphed into the perfume of summer sunshine and wildflowers. A weed in the cracked asphalt began to grow, reaching toward me. "I only wish to comfort his lover."

"I'm going back in." I stepped around Andy. Aurora grabbed my arm.

Moss took the other. "Sorry," he said, "but I can't let you. If the master vampire believes it's too dangerous for you—"

I jerked and squirmed, trying to get out of their combined hold. "Let go," I commanded. "Andy, help me!"

My power to compel was not the same as that of an Undead's and typically only seemed to work on humans. My friends were anything but. Andy gave me a *you've got to be kidding* glance. "We should leave."

My new plant friend came to my rescue, weaving itself around Moss' ankles and yanking him off his feet. Without his iron hold on me, I managed to shove Aurora away. She crashed into Andy. I marched past the Fae and back inside.

Ozmeus caught up to me inside. "Wait here," he said, pointing to the shadows near the restroom. An ancient pay phone was beeping, the dangling receiver having been abandoned during the mass exodus. I paused, listening to the voices coming from the main room. They sounded jovial and relaxed, the tinkling lilt of the princess interwoven among them. "Why did some patrons not flee, while others did?" I asked.

He leaned close to my ear, his warm breath on my neck. "They know they aren't in danger of becoming a plaything for the Undead."

Moss swept in, a thundering, pissed off vamp, and

lifted me from my feet. He tossed me over his shoulder and the sudden shift made me cry out. But the sound was swallowed by the flood of Killion's nest who swarmed the place. The last thing I saw, besides Moss' backside, was Katarina, Killion's enforcer, snapping her fingers and giving nonverbal orders to the others. She plastered on a bored expression, after she scowled at me, and sauntered into the main room.

The Fae prince had already disappeared.

As Aurora cursed me in a foreign language, probably putting a spell on me, and Moss dumped me unceremoniously into the backseat of the limo, Andy dove in.

We drove over the crushed gravel of the lot and I saw Killion through the bar's front window. Spiked Hair was across from him in the booth. The two looked friendly enough, but even from this distance, I sensed Killion's tightly controlled emotions. Power oozed off him and I shivered. He sensed my gaze, but he didn't glance my way, nor say anything telepathically. His nest had filled the place, and the newcomers were outnumbered, which made me no less pissed at being ushered off, but slightly less fearful.

As Aurora chastised me, I refocused on the leader of the other nest. The woman from the bus was half in his lap, raking her fingers through his spiked hair. While he didn't give any indication he knew I was sending daggers his way, she did, turning her head to meet my eyes.

In that briefest of moments before Moss sped us away, she smiled, flashing a set of fangs.

Not a human, then. Another vampire.

She winked.

A wave of her Undead magic hit the vehicle, but the protective ward Killion had placed on it reflected it back to her. I twisted in the seat to watch out the rear and saw her flinch. A tiny, nearly imperceptible reaction, but I smiled ruefully. "Who are they?" I called to Moss.

Hitting the county road, he accelerated. The landscape whooshed past. "Evil."

I tried to catch his attention in the rearview mirror. "I need more context than that."

Tiny worry lines appeared at the corners of his deep brown eyes. He paused and gripped the steering wheel tight enough to bend it. "We do not speak their name."

Name, singular. I glanced at Aurora and lowered my voice. "But they're just vampires, right?"

"Not *only*," Moss said. Of course he'd heard my question with his enhanced faculties. "They are..."

When he didn't finish, Aurora sighed. "The official term is *štrigon*." Moss tried to interrupt but she ignored him and continued. He crossed himself. "Uses of the label are, for the most part, based on a scant few unconfirmed sources or records from hundreds of years ago, containing more creative license than actual fact. Many claim the concept of modern vampirism is based on these 'again-walkers,' although we know the Undead have existed since the beginning of time. Štrigon are often lumped in with a particular type of witch who obtains human infants to work spells, and somewhat inaccurately interchanged with zombies, due to the whole rising from the dead and consuming the blood and flesh of their victims."

Lovely. "So a specialized branch of the Undead."

"They follow the old ways," Moss said quietly. "We do not interact with them. Ever."

Yet, Killion was doing exactly that at the moment. "Why did he stay?" I questioned the driver. "And why did that guy call him 'brother'? He has no siblings, right?"

"They were part of the same nest in New Orleans. It was a long time ago."

Vampires often referred to their nest mates as brother or sister.

It seemed like it carried some type of message, though. "You know him?"

The driver flashed his fangs. "Only by reputation."

Andy looked sick. I sort of felt that way, too. "It's not a good one, I take it."

"The master stayed to make sure you got away. Whatever Lasarus is planning, you must not fall under his control."

I exchanged a glance with Aurora. "Why would I?"

She shook her head, signaling she didn't know.

Moss did. "For as long as I can remember, he's hunted reapers." His eyes, vampire red, held mine in the reflection. "He wants his soul back, and you're a way for him to get it."

FIVE

"How?" I was a grim with necromancy powers, but I wasn't in charge of souls. "He'd have to work that out with SMG. There's nothing I can do for him."

Soul Management Group handled soul contracts and reincarnation. Those humans who'd sought out vampirism had given up their soul to become such, unlike Killion who'd been born with one. Because he'd had one human parent, it was possible his was still present, but we weren't a hundred-percent sure. Death refused to tell me or him on principle. He hated the Undead.

"He's unusual," Moss said. We neared downtown and he slowed. "When he kills a reaper, he traps their soul and feeds on it for months, even years, allowing him to have one for that time. He accesses a trifecta of power —human, grim, and vampire. He's a legend. No other Undead has ever acquired such potent magic."

"Feeds on their soul?" I shuddered.

"And you're Grim Zero." Aurora looked scared. "If

he traps yours and feeds on it, he may be able to transfer it to himself." She sat forward. "Could that be why he's here? To challenge Killion for her?"

The hotel came into view. Andy fiddled with the button to lower the window and sucked in air. "Tonight has not gone the way I anticipated."

"He hasn't come through these parts in decades," Moss said. "I doubt it's a social call."

Now I leaned forward as we pulled into the massive curving drive. "Take me back. Killion could be in trouble."

The hotel bellhop, along with two bodyguard vampires Killion had recently hired, emerged from inside. They headed straight for my door.

Moss turned to peer at me over his seat. "My orders stand—protect you at all costs. I will not be swayed, so don't think threatening me will do any good."

I'd manipulated him previously into disobeying Killion, and although he hadn't gotten in trouble, thanks to my cajoling his master into forgiving him, he'd made it clear that in the future, he'd do anything for me, with the exception of outright disobedience.

The door opened and I was hauled out and into the hotel, my protests dying on the wind.

"Put me down," I demanded of the Undead carrying me over his shoulder. No one but other vampires noticed us, his magic making us invisible to humans. Andy and Aurora hurried to keep up as the brute strode through the lobby and into the glass elevator.

He unceremoniously dumped me onto my feet. "Master said I couldn't use compulsion on you." His gruff voice matched his enormous biceps, both of which suggested he was always up for fisticuffs, and he was none too happy about not being allowed to employ his vampire abilities on me. "But to use any other means necessary to keep you safe."

His partner, also of the Beefy Biceps and Fight-Ready Club, squeezed into the space, nearly crushing my friends. He offered a smile, but since it was heavy on fangs, it did little to suggest he was friendly. "We're here to act as your shield from harm, ma'am."

"Did you just *ma'am* me?" His smile faded under my glare. "I'm twenty-four, and a long way from—"

Aurora squeezed my arm. "Thank you," she interrupted. Andy hooked an arm around her waist, drawing her close, but she shouldered him back an inch. "You'll have to be patient with her. It's been a stressful night."

I ground my teeth. "Do not ever call me that again," I told the guard. In my head, I nicknamed him Tweedle Dee. "You should be protecting Killion, not me."

Both of them snorted. Tweedle Dee said, "The Master is more than capable of handling the interlopers."

His companion, Tweedle Dum, agreed with a head bob. "He can take care of them, trust me."

I wanted to. The elevator stopped and we peeled ourselves out of it. Pennyworth threw open the door to the penthouse. "Thank the Undead gods you are safe, Miss Chloe."

I patted his shoulder as I passed by him. "Undead gods? I didn't realize there was such a thing." I shrugged off my coat and he took it from me, hanging it up. Ghost rushed to greet me and I hugged her, then ogled at the living area. "What did you do?"

In the time we'd been gone, the furniture had been switched out from Killion's brooding castle in Romania-type decor to a sleek, modern ivory ensemble. "Is it too much?"

I ran a hand over the back of a sofa, the buttery soft fabric making me forget any impending danger for a second. I bent to lay my cheek against it. "It's beautiful."

"Italian leather." Pennyworth beamed. "It seemed young and fresh. Master is long overdue for an update."

Killion would hate it. "I love it." The antique coffee table had been replaced as well, but not the main attraction—Killion's favorite chair. It stood out like a sore thumb, with its ornate wooden back and arms. There was no getting rid of it, however—it had belonged to his father in Romania.

The butler followed my gaze, worrying his hands. "It doesn't fit, does it?"

"Not in the least." But we both knew it was here to stay. I sat on the sofa, trying it out, and hugged a generous sized throw pillow as I sank into the cushions. Kicking off my boots, I sunk my toes into the plush rug he'd also added, and sighed at the sumptuous feel of it all. The pattern had waves of different shades of blue that reminded me of the ocean.

"I placed the former set in storage for safe keeping," Pennyworth said, his face morphing back and forth between joy over my obvious love of the grouping and worry over Killion's dislike of it.

I knew plenty of ways to gain the master vampire's

acceptance of the new furnishings, and wasn't above using my pull with him to do it. "As long as he has his chair, he'll come around. I'll make sure of it."

"What a lovely update." Aurora tested the opposite sofa, appreciating the cushiony and supple leather. "I'm sad for the cows who donated to it, but it's exquisite."

Andy massaged her shoulders and she closed her eyes. His pupils were big and he oozed a wolfish carnality. "Maybe we should go back to your place...?"

Her lids popped open and she shot off the couch. "Um, we should help Chloe first."

Right. I tossed the pillow aside and scratched Ghost behind the ears when she took its place in my lap. "I need everything you have on the *štrigon*," I said to Pennyworth.

"Why? Is that what the code red was about?"

I nodded. "A few blew into town tonight. What do you know about them?"

"They are formidable. Nothing to mess with." He began scanning the top most bookshelves, where some of the oldest volumes rested. "While I always encourage acquiring knowledge, I hesitate to do so with recklessness. You're not going to attempt anything ill advised, are you?"

The beefy brothers returned to the hallway to remain outside the door. Andy slouched on the sofa Aurora had vacated.

"I'm not reckless."

He lifted a brow to let me know he disagreed. He'd been around for plenty of my not so smart adventures. "I have your word you will not leave here until the master says you can?"

Ghost barked, wagging her tail. The dog knew he had me. "Sure."

"Let me see both of your hands."

Reapers keepers. Once again, he had me dead to rights. I uncrossed the fingers behind my back and raised both hands in the air. "I give you my word. Happy now?"

He grinned and returned to surveying the shelves.

Aurora scanned the books alongside him. "You own an impressive collection. Not as extensive as mine in witchcraft, but otherwise comprehensive."

"Perhaps you will assist me with improving that category."

"I'd be delighted to."

"Can we get back to the *štrigon?*" I asked.

Pennyworth handed me three volumes. "In modern day, we refer to them as strigoi."

I dropped into Killion's chair to start reading. The master vampire's scent wrapped around me, and I sent him a mental message. *Are you all right?*

It took a moment before his reply: *I will be home soon.*

Not an answer, but it would have to do. I didn't want to read—I wanted to start swinging my scythe and making heads roll. This time I had to let my partner handle things.

Andy got up, wrapped his arms around Aurora, and began nuzzling her neck. She trailed her fingers over the spines seductively, as if she were focused on him. He murmured something in her ear and she softened against him. The Fae magic lingered on us, a coating of sensuality and seduction.

Powerful magic, to be sure. Their touching sent out a ripple of need, of desire. It was faint, but strong enough to tease at my own skin.

As if a switch had been tripped, Aurora pivoted in the shifter's hold to kiss him. They suddenly began grasping at each other, and Pennyworth hesitated in his search for a surprised beat, then continued selecting volumes for me, as if nothing were out of the ordinary.

"Get a room," I grumbled at my hyped-up friends. "Seriously. It's a hotel, they have plenty."

I accepted the next stack from the butler and began flipping through them, looking for information about this group of vampires. The first I opened was in another language, handwritten like many of Aurora's ancient grimoires. Thanks to a spell she'd previously worked on me, my eyes adjusted and the words morphed into English.

As I studied a section, Aurora and Andy slipped from the penthouse, her giggling all the way.

SIX

My skin felt too tight, my body needing to move to work off the energy and anxiety, but I needed to know as much as I could about this new threat in town.

Pennyworth brought me a cup of warmed cider, and took time to point out certain chapters in the books. He seemed to know a lot about them.

"Have you encountered them before?" I asked.

He wouldn't meet my eyes. "In the old country."

"Have you been with Killion since he moved here from Romania?"

"I have been employed by his family a very long while." He turned an opened book around, showing me a painted picture of a beast attacking a human. "They have evolved over time, much like the rest of us, so as to go undetected. It's best to give them space, stay out of their way, and pray they move on soon. They may leave a path of destruction in their wake, but there's nothing we can do to stop them."

First the Fae. Now these ultra-vamps. "This is my territory. Killion's. No one gets to come here and wreak havoc for their own purposes."

My blood warmed suddenly, and I put down the volume I held, coming to my feet. "Killion..."

I ran to the door and threw it open. My heart gave a leap. He looked like a summer storm ready to break over Danté's Grove, but when he saw me, his dark countenance lifted. He smiled—a rare sight—and held out his arms.

I rushed into them, hugging him tight. "I was so worried. Are you okay?"

Tweedle Dee spoke up. "All is well, master."

"Thank you." He led me inside and closed the door. "There's no need for such concern."

His tense energy suggested that was an exaggeration.

Pennyworth greeted and assisted him with his coat. He hung it up and scurried to the kitchen—possibly to create a meal, or simply to avoid Killion's reaction to the new living room furniture.

My skin buzzed with desire, the Fae magic swirling around him and invading my senses. He barely gave it a second glance as I led him into the room, pausing in mid-step, instantly aware of my climbing desire. His eyes glittered with a matching lust.

Pennyworth returned, a glass of Killion's favorite wine in hand. The master vampire accepted it, eyeing me over the rim as he sipped. He licked his lips and handed it to me. "Take the rest of the evening off, Pennyworth. I'll call you if we have need of you."

The butler barely made it out the door before I

launched myself into Killion's arms. In an attempt to set the glass down first, the wine splashed out, the beautiful goblet shattering on the floor as he caught me and carried me to his bedroom.

I would need to apologize to the butler in the morning, but finally, *finally*, I could satisfy my craving for my mate and his magic.

Desire wove between us like an infinity sign, our individual desires accentuating the others and ratcheting up our need. We ripped each other's clothing off, tangling together, arms and legs, lips and breath. He carried me to the mattress, laid me down, and worshipped me.

Since our first bonding, it was always like this—we entered a state of pure awareness and bliss from the combining of our physical bodies.

The intensity was enough to rattle the windows and shake the building. The Fae magic only sweetened the already incredible bond we shared. For hours, we sustained the state of bliss, finding new ways to love one another into it. Each time I thought I was fully satiated, a simple look or touch from him would start it all over again. I could not get enough of him, nor he of me.

The sun striped the sky when I finally insisted on eating. I needed fuel, and he had yet to tell me what had transpired between him and the strigoi.

Like a married couple, we fished through the contents of the refrigerator and pantry. I started a pot of coffee and he made eggs. "I'm not much of a cook," he admitted. "I can call Pennyworth if you are in need of a large breakfast."

I placed slices of bread in the toaster slots, then

wrapped my arms around him at the stove, the spatula in his hand. "I rather like this domestic side of you." I kissed his naked back, his dragon tattoo on full display.

That's all it took. Before I knew it, I was seated on the counter, and he was pushing between my knees. The eggs burned, the toast was forgotten.

When we came up for air much later, I went to the bathroom to shower, riding a high due to his magic and the pleasure he'd brought. But I was weak from the physical activity and lack of sustenance. He joined me, washing my hair and tucking me into bed afterward, the sounds of Pennyworth in the kitchen trickling in as I nestled down. "I'll be back with a proper breakfast for you," he said, dropping a kiss on my forehead. "Rest."

While I was exhausted and starving, his absence made it impossible to do so. It seemed I couldn't have him out of my sight without feeling irritable. Like a roller coaster, my emotions swung between the all-consuming euphoria and a raging lust that no amount of intimacy could quench.

I studied the flames in the fireplace, wishing I had the books about the strigoi. I also needed my phone. The only reason I didn't jump up and find both was the fact I didn't have the strength to do so.

Which freaked me out. I'd always recovered from our marathon bouts of lovemaking as rapidly as my body healed, although previously I had devoured plenty of food as well. While Killion rarely tired, I still did. I required less sleep than previously, but I needed a few hours every night, and there was no bottom to my endless hunger. Much like there was none to my craving for him.

This had to be more than the aftereffects of the Fae magic. Memories of the bar and the way I'd acted when the princess approached made me wince. Death would be none too happy I'd screwed up the investigation, but it couldn't be fixed at the moment.

Those thoughts circled me around to what had played out afterward and I sank deeper into the covers, reliving the high points. It felt incredible to let go and just be me with someone. The contentment returned, not as intense, but more of a subtle buzz along my limbs and in my chest. *Hurry*, I mentally told Killion. *I need you.*

He appeared in the doorway with a tray. As if he'd read my earlier thoughts as well—which he probably had—two of the books, along with my phone, accompanied a carafe of coffee and cups. "I sense you are not resting as instructed."

I chuckled. "My body is, just not my mind. I need to check on Aurora, and you have to fill me in about your friends."

Setting the tray on the table in the reading nook, he frowned. "They are not friends." He crossed the floor on silent feet, handing me a mug. "Coffee first."

I struggled to sit up, my limbs heavy. He had to help me, his frown deepening. Once I was able to hold the cup and sip, he returned to the tray to pour one for himself. "You are truly weak? Do you need my blood?"

The scent of the brew calmed me. "It appears you've finally worn me out. But honestly? If you were to so much as look at me the right way, I'd drag myself over there to jump your bones."

Bringing his drink with him, he climbed in beside me.

"It is the bond between us. I feel it, too, this craving that defies all else."

"For you, it's not simply my grim blood?"

He stroked my arm. "This goes beyond that. Beyond anything I've known or ever heard of."

Even as he hugged me to him, the burning ache under the surface of my skin flared. "It's all consuming," I muttered, turning my head to stare at his lips.

He caught mine with a coffee-laced kiss. My world tilted and I started to crawl into his lap, my hand shaking as I set my drink on the nightstand.

Or tried to, anyway. I missed and the porcelain cup crashed to the floor, spilling coffee on the rug.

"Oh, I'm sorry," I said, but honestly didn't care. All I wanted was to kiss him again.

Killion groaned, setting down his own and grabbing my arms to hold me back. "You're too weak. You must rest."

Pennyworth bustled in, wheeling a silver cart filled with plates of food. "Pardon, master." He kept his eyes lowered. "Shall I come back later?"

"Leave the cart," Killion grumbled, maneuvering me off his lap.

"I'm so sorry about the spilled wine, and, now coffee," I said as the butler fled.

"No worries," he called.

Killion stood, dodging my grasping hand. "Chloe, you must eat."

"Yes," I said, licking my lips. The assortment of items smelled delicious, yet I couldn't take my focus off the vampire. "I must."

The frown was back, deeper than ever. He loaded a plate of my favorites and brought it to the bed. "I have never compelled you, but if you do not obey me and eat everything on this, I will be forced to do so."

I didn't believe him. "No, you won't."

"You will have more strength for other things once you refuel." A bribe.

"Always so logical." I consumed everything in minutes. Killion watched in fascination. "Talk," I demanded around a bite of buttery toast, already feeling better. "Tell me about the strigoi."

He stole a slice of my bacon and I growled. Smiling, he took a bite, then fed me the rest.

As I finished the lavish meal, he told me a tale I wished were fiction.

SEVEN

"The strigoi of the Grimm Brothers tales is loosely based on fact." His focus was on the flames in the hearth, but his violet eyes were a million miles away. "What those leave out is how close vampires and witches used to be. Not the white witches and healers, but those who worked with blood and death. They were allies, and the Undead profited from their spells."

I drank some coffee. "Aurora never mentioned that. I thought all vampires and witches hated each other."

"Historically, no. A group of my kind sought the power her ancestors held. They wished to look beyond the veil and discover a way to retrieve their lost souls."

"Is that possible?"

"Not that I'm aware of, but it has not stopped them from trying. As we both know, magic can change, and there are many of the old ways that have been forgotten, lost, throughout time. Who knows what the ancient ones could or could not achieve?"

Death knew. SMG knew. I'd need to ask a few questions of my boss and his.

Killion toyed with a second slice of bacon. I'd purposely left it for him, not because I didn't want it and he did, but because feeding each other, the act of sharing food, symbolized so much more in his world than in the human one.

He broke it in two, handing me the larger section. Such a simple act, but filled with meaning—I was his to watch over, to care for, in every way. "What changed between the two?"

"The strigoi turned on the witches, causing mass hunts of their kind."

I munched on the bacon. *Perfection.* It was the exact crispness I loved. "No wonder they hate the Undead."

"Indeed. A small faction tainted the alliance and it has never recovered. It is one of the reasons none in the supernatural community trust us."

"The ones at the bar? They're the originals who ruined it for the rest of you?"

"Only Lasarus. The others with him came much later. He created them."

"Why is he here?"

I held my breath at his hesitation. With our bond, he could keep few things from me, yet he still tried to shelter me. "The occurrences of the past four months have stirred up a good many in our world. Your power has grown tremendously and it acts as a beacon."

Moss had told me the truth. "He's after me."

"I will protect you, although"—he grinned, anticipating my argument. One we had regularly—"you are more than capable of handling yourself."

"If you believed that, you wouldn't have had Moss and your bodyguards cart me off like a trussed-up goose. He's lucky I didn't shock him with my necromancy." Many of the Undead feared I'd "raise" their souls and turn them back into humans. It didn't work that way, but their fear and gossip worked in my favor, so I hadn't put any energy into disavowing them of the notion.

"My protective streak got the best of me. I prefer to keep you as far from that group as possible. While I believe in your amazing abilities, four of them against only you may prove to be your downfall."

I pinched his cheek lightly. "But I have you and Aurora, and my contract isn't up yet. Death won't let anything happen to me."

His eyes crinkled in the corners and he gripped my hand. "Let's not test that theory. As I recall he nearly killed you himself at the new year."

My boss and I had a complicated relationship. Some days, he was as protective as Killion. Others, he seemed determined to sabotage me.

After the master vampire and I had created our binding, Death had claimed he and Grim Zero, my original incarnation, had shared the same soul-yoking. While I felt a connection to him, it was nothing like what existed between me and Killion. "He claims he can't kill, only manage those of us who harvest their souls. Do you believe him?"

"No."

Okay then. "Me either, but I'd bet money he won't

allow the strigoi to get me. If anyone is going to shorten my lifespan, he'll want the honors."

The simple mention of such an event made Killion's magic rise and ripple over me. "He tries any such thing and I will break down the very walls of hell to end him."

And that was an *incatusa sufletum*-bound vampire for you. "I love you," I said, kissing him. My normal energy was returning. "What of the Fae? Did either give up any evidence about the attacks?"

"Regarding that." He rose and whisked the tray of empty plates off the bed. Next, he refilled my coffee, and I waited for him to go on.

Accepting it, I reclined on the plump pillows. The lascivious look he gave me suggested he wanted to distract me with other things. I returned it with one of my own, but prompted, "Tell me."

He trailed his hand over my shin, up my thigh. "I no longer believe either Ozmeus nor his cousin, the princess, are behind the attacks."

"Then who is?" His fingers stilled. At the change in his expression, my rising libido sank. "You're kidding," I said, reading his mind.

A longing-filled, salacious glance at my legs, and then, "Afraid not. I felt it at the bar. Lasarus has learned a new skill, I believe."

"Which is?"

"The strigoi can drain their victims' blood, but they can now do more. Much, much more."

The nape of my neck prickled in warning. I thought about the papery skin of our corpses. The looks of agony on their faces. I sat up once more, anger filling me. "Suck all the fluid from their bodies?"

"Not only that."

"What else is there?"

A muscle in his jaw twitched. "He is draining them of their very life essence."

EIGHT

I had a new target to bring to heel.

But first, I had the morning shift at The Bean.

"Mason will cover for you," Killion insisted. His young protégée was like him in many ways—half-vampire, half-human. Intelligent. Yet so, so young. We both worked at the local coffee shop and I had trained the kid. "You should stay here."

I stood in his luxurious bathroom, raking my hair into a high ponytail. Normally I braided it, but lately that style didn't seem to fit as well. "I have a life, and I'm not hiding from the strigoi. If they come after me, they'll get a big surprise."

Killion had alerted Death, and as soon as we had the go-ahead, we'd proceed with whatever SMG required we do to bring them to justice. The Fae were another matter —I didn't like them hanging in the area, but didn't have reason at this point to make them leave.

I grabbed my stun gun from the counter and was taking my scythe with me, too. Passing by my mostly naked boyfriend lounging in the doorway, it was all I could do not to jump him again. I was going to be late as it was. "Meanwhile, I'll be fully armed, and you'll be skulking around keeping an eye on me."

"I do not skulk."

I dropped a light kiss on his perfect, full lips. "Of course you do. You're a pro at it, and I love you for it."

He growled and snatched me up, making me cry out with laughter. "Come back to bed, Grim. I'll show you what I'm a pro at."

I was indeed late for work, but Mason was there when I arrived. He had the machines warmed up, cookies from my Aunt Camille unpacked and in the cases, and the front supplies fully stocked and ready to go. Pop music played over the speaker system, and the body-guards, Tweedle Dee and Tweedle Dum, stood at the back exit.

"This is overkill, don't you think?" I challenged the master vampire who'd accompanied me inside. "Your henchmen will scare away customers, and Mason is still a kid. Besides, he has school."

"Hey," the youth said, resentment clear in his tone. "I volunteered to be here. Don't look a gift vampire in the tooth. And it's Saturday." He rolled his eyes in a "duh" manner.

Killion stared down my annoyance. "I've lived longer than you and know better than to underestimate the strigoi." He was hyper-vigilant these days about every-thing after his right hand lieutenant had betrayed him a few months back. "You are a powerful creature, but allow me my indulgences. I can and will do all in my power to protect what is mine."

"Word choice," I reminded him. "Creature sounds like a horror movie monster."

He planted a kiss on my mouth and headed for the door. "The henchmen have names—Mags and Cron. Do not harass them. They are doing my bidding, as is Mason."

"Mags and what? Did their mothers pick those straight out of Names for Vampire Bodyguards?"

He pinned me with an exasperated look. "Until I understand the extent of the strigoi's new abilities, we must use extra caution."

"But you're here, it's broad daylight, and I'll be surrounded by people. They won't make a move against me." I pointed at the two-person table at the far back. "I suppose you plan to occupy your favorite booth all morning?"

"And get you in trouble again with your boss?" He shook his head. "I have an investor meeting to attend. You're in capable hands, therefore, I am off to skulk while I run my empire."

"Funny," I called after him. Because he didn't eat or drink much, and we needed that space when we got busy, Wade had told me my boyfriend could only stay for an hour max during any given shift. When I'd shared that with Killion, he'd vowed to buy the place and send Wade packing. I still wasn't sure if I'd convinced him not to. "See you tonight."

It was good Mason was there. Nita had a migraine and I told her to stay home when she called in. He wasn't as experienced with customers, but he charmed most with his natural vamp allure and every single one left happy and fully caffeinated. "Is Megan working at the clinic today?" he asked during a slump.

He didn't know? Hmm. The two texted constantly. If she hadn't told him she was free, maybe she didn't want him to know. It hadn't been that long since I was a teenager, but it felt like a lifetime ago. "I don't recall," I lied and started cleaning the soda machine.

Aurora dropped by mid-morning. "Sorry about last night."

I waved it off and fixed her favorite drink, adding a muffin to go for her. We walked to the exit, and I lowered my voice, even though no one paid us any attention. "You didn't mention the reason you hate vampires is due to the strigoi."

Her attention riveted on the cup in her hand. "It's a part of history witches don't like to talk about."

Understandable. "If you ever do want to, I'm here." I wondered if she realized Lasarus was one of the originals who'd betrayed her kind. "I'm going after them."

Her green eyes met mine. "Why?"

"We believe they're responsible for the arboretum killings, not the Fae. I need proof, but once I get it, they're gone."

She scrunched up her nose. "They're a powerful lot. You need to be careful. I thought you said the victims had been sucked dry of all life."

"Apparently, Lasarus has learned a new trick."

Her eyes hardened. "I'll be more than happy to bring the strigoi down."

"The Scooby Gang rides again." We bumped fists.

"We need a different name for our group."

I laughed. "I think it's rather apt."

No trouble showed up after she left, not even Death, and I lost myself in the familiar rhythm of pulling shots from Ambrosia, my favorite espresso machine, and keeping the display case stocked with yummy goodness. Technically, I didn't need this job, but I wanted it. It was a normal piece of my very *not* normal life.

When I took my break midmorning, I dove into a compendium of spellery Aurora had left with me, my mind blown at the simplicity of a binding spell. It was temporary, and I planned to try it the next time I encountered a noncompliant soul who didn't want me to reap them. I was practicing drawing the sigil for it when Mason burst through the door of the back room. "That SMG dude is here."

"Death?"

He shook his head. "The weird guy with the accent."

'Weird' covered most SMG employees. "Can you be more specific?"

But he was already gone. Putting a bookmark in the compendium, I tucked it in my bag out of sight. Peering through the window of the swinging door, I cased the counter area and then the seating section. Well, to give the kid credit, he wasn't wrong about the label.

Tinder, the weirdo in question and SMG's contract manager, met my gaze and motioned me out. He typically carried a blood oath book and a cigarette lighter that he nervously toyed with. Well over six feet and angular, even under his wool coat, his usual newspaper boy hat was missing and his hair stood at odd angles as if he'd raked his hands through it again and again. "I'll take a double shot and a blueberry muffin," he said in his cockney accent as I approached.

"I'm not your waitress. Get in line at the counter like everyone else." Assuming he was there to convey orders from SMG, I glanced around to be sure no one was watching. The rush had slowed and our current customers consisted of college students mainlining caffeine, and a pair of older men chatting over crosswords and black coffees. I wiped at the table, even though it was clean and lowered my voice. "What's the word on apprehending our suspects? And why are you here instead of Death?"

"The big sot is busy, and this assignment has nothing to do with those murders."

I straightened and shoved the towel in the pocket of my apron. My stomach sunk a bit. He had to be here on behalf of Mei Han. "Oh." I slid into the chair across from him. Mason watched us carefully and I gave him a reassuring smile. "What *does* it have to do with?"

He played with his metal lighter, flipping the lid open and closed over and over. "There's a ghost in the machine. We need you to exorcise it, Grave Girl."

"I've asked you not to call me that." My telepathic link to Killion opened and I sensed him tuning in. "What are you talking about?"

The lid of the lighter flung open. Closed. "We have a ghost problem."

"At SMG?" I glanced around, once more making sure no one was eavesdropping. "What kind?"

"Are you daft? A haunting. What other is there?"

"Soul Management Group is haunted?" I laughed. The head of SMG and I had a rocky relationship. She had to be desperate to send for me. "I bet Mei loves that."

"It's no laughing matter." Tinder paused his neurotic flipping. "Things are screwy. Contracts are on hold. Souls are backing up and being routed to the wrong incarnation. Your assistance is mandatory."

Was this why I hadn't seen Death in days? "Surely there are more experienced reapers to handle it."

"Mei requested you." He said it with a sense of resigned disbelief, as though he couldn't understand it himself. "Said it was your responsibility."

I don't like it, Killion said telepathically.

Me either. My sixth sense tingled with suspicion. "Why would it be *my* responsibility? Who is this ghost?"

"How should I know? Mei told me to come get you, so here I am."

"And how are you supposed to transport me to SMG?" It was after all part of the great beyond. While I had once seen a hologram of Mei at her desk, I couldn't visualize what the place looked like. It was an alternate dimension but did it resemble heaven, the fictional Ministry of Magic in the Harry Potter movies, or something else entirely?

"You ask too many questions."

Killion chuckled in my head. It was an ongoing complaint of his as well.

I ignored my partner and pinned Tinder with an icy glare. "Until those questions are answered to my satisfaction, and I'm fully apprised of what I'm getting myself into, Mei is on her own. Besides, I have work. I can't just take off at her command."

Tinder gave a dry laugh, as if I were joking. "You don't have a choice."

Mags and Cron appeared, taking up their post on either side of the swinging door to the back. They also glared at him and I knew Killion had sent them to make sure this didn't go sideways.

I rose at the jingle from behind me, signifying a new customer. "Give Mei my regards."

Returning to the counter, I shooed the bodyguards to the back so they didn't scare off the pair of moms pushing their toddlers in strollers. The two were frazzled, in need of their favorite beverage and some adult bonding.

Tinder got in line behind them and I smirked to myself. In my head, Killion said: *It might be wise for you to spend time at SMG.*

Me: *You just said you didn't like the idea.*

Killion: *You could bond with Mei. Get an extension on your contract.*

My strategic boyfriend had a point. It wasn't a horrible idea, except for the fact Mei and I would *never* bond. Never ever. I also sensed he was now pushing for it because of another reason.

Me: *You know you can't keep secrets from me.*

Killion's response was a heavy sigh, then silence.

I worked on the iced lattes, adding extra whipped cream on top. Mothers of young children deserved it, in my opinion.

Me: *I'm not hiding from the strigoi.*

Killion: *You will be untouchable at SMG. It would relieve my worries.*

And there it was—the real motivation for his change of heart.

Me: *Have faith, vampire master. I'd rather take on your frenemies than Mei Han.*

A long pause. *As you wish.*

The link went dead. Okay then. Mason took payment from the women and Tinder stepped forward. He placed his order with a side of Glare At Chloe, then retreated to his table.

He was still there when the twins, Shane and Kenner, arrived to relieve us. I had to give him props for tenacity.

I called Nita to check on her while I made drinks for my staff at the clinic. She was already feeling better and promised to stop by Frosty Paws later to chat. After saying goodbye to her, I slipped out the back exit, avoiding the SMG operative.

I cut through an alleyway to get to my car. The body-guards followed at a respectful distance and I ignored them. At home, Ghost and Corvus, Aurora's raven who'd adopted me, greeted me and I took them off Vera's hands, delivering mint green tea to my landlady in exchange for her pet sitting. The animals and I then headed to the vet clinic in my new-to-me convertible.

Grave Girl—yes, I'd named her, and no, I hadn't told a soul that I'd used the nickname I claimed to hate but secretly liked—was ten years old and had a few dings. I loved her regardless. She was all mine, and I'd paid for a new top and replaced the balding tires. The engine needed an overhaul, she leaked oil, and sometimes she struggled to start even though Moss had replaced the battery.

Temperamental or caused by my roller coaster magic, I wasn't sure. Since I'd tapped into my powers, certain electrical and mechanical systems went haywire around me on occasion. Aurora said it probably was a side effect of the intense energy I generated whenever I was emotional.

Patty, my office manager, was humming in between calls and patients arriving for appointments. It was another new thing since my bonding with Killion—I'd taken to doing it as well. I always had times when I heard music in my head, and my mom had hummed when she worked. Hearing Patty jamming along with whatever playlist she'd put on the clinic speakers brought me immense joy.

I handed her a latte with white chocolate syrup, and she made prayer hands as a thank you before answering the ringing phone.

Securing Corvus on his perch behind her desk, Ghost raced to the front window where she loved to sleep and watch the passersby.

After storing my coat and backpack in my locker, I passed Dr. O'Leary in the hall, said good morning by way of handing him a black coffee, and grabbed a file folder outside one of the exam rooms.

Time to go to work again.

NINE

A lady came in with a nine-year-old poodle mix who hadn't eaten in several days and looked miserable. In the exam room, I took down the information the owner provided, but didn't need to palpate the poor dog's abdomen to discover her bladder was swollen near to bursting. I nabbed O'Leary the moment he finished with his patient and handed him the file. "Bladder stones," I told him. "The dog needs surgery now."

"You're not licensed yet," he admonished. "Don't diagnose or prescribe."

He was right—I wasn't, but my magic didn't need an official framed certificate hanging on the office wall to know what the majority of our patients needed. It told me.

He was human, a mundane. I couldn't explain that to him without him advising me to see a psychiatrist. "Please confirm my findings while I prep the surgical unit."

Leaving him scowling, I went to do just that.

Andy came through the back entrance looking as surly as I felt. "Need to talk to you."

He worked part-time for me as a tech. "Has to wait. I've got a poodle ready to burst her bladder. Thanks so much for bailing on me last night."

He huffed, clearly exasperated. "Give me a minute and I'll scrub in."

He disappeared and returned at the same time O'Leary found me and conceded my diagnosis was accurate. "You seem to have an innate sense about animals."

Ha! "You could say that."

"Want me to get the dog?" Andy asked.

I nodded. "Room three. Be careful when you pick her up. She's in pain."

O'Leary went to the sink to scrub. "I didn't see him on the schedule for today."

I helped him with his gloves. "I don't know how long he can stay, but from the looks of our waiting room, we can use the extra set of hands."

The procedure went off without a hitch, the doctor removing three stones, one the size of a marble and sporting nasty spikes. When the poodle mix was in recovery, I assured her waiting and very relieved owner that all was well and met Andy out back.

Because the clinic was downtown, we only had a small fenced yard. Our neighbors had the same sized lots, but they had turned them into parking spaces for employees and renters. Andy lived above the clinic but he didn't own a vehicle. Since we had a plot of grass for our patients to pee in, everyone had to park in the municipal lot a block over. He and a short woman loitered at the far end of the area, near the gate, as if they were ready to bolt. Due to the fact Mags and Cron were glaring at them from their posts at the door, I couldn't say I blamed them.

The woman was dark haired with haunted eyes that widened slightly when she saw me. She'd bowed her head when I approached. "You came."

"Sure," I said to her. Without glancing at the hulking muscle behind me, I spoke to Mags and Cron. "Make yourselves scarce. I'm in no danger."

For as big as they were, they moved as soundlessly as most supernaturals. Andy nodded appreciation once they were out of sight. With their vampire hearing, and the fact they hadn't gone far, we all knew they could still eavesdrop, but their absence gave the illusion of privacy. "How can I help you?"

The woman flicked her gaze to Andy, who gave another nod, this one encouraging.

Her dark gaze dropped to the ground. "Ever since that day, I have cravings. I can't sleep. I hear...dead things."

Totally lost, I wasn't sure where to start. She had begun shaking, out of fear or something else, I wasn't sure. "How about we start with introductions? I'm Chloe. What do you prefer to be called?"

Names held power. Supernaturals never willingly offered their true identity to anyone they didn't know or deeply trust. They could be compelled into all sorts of ugly actions by the entity using it. "Pepper," she said, and raised her head to meet my gaze. "You don't remember me?"

"You were in your coyote form." Andy patted her back. "She's a grim, remember? Lots of magic, but she doesn't have the scent abilities you and I possess."

"Coyote?" An involuntary shiver rippled down my spine. I reflexively touched my arm where one had bitten me in December. It was all I could do not to step back. "You're one of them."

Her face paled and random tufts of hair sprouted on her face, neck, and hands. She held them out in supplication. "I'm so sorry. I didn't realize who you were. I was only protecting the safe house."

I understood, and I also knew why she was here. She'd tasted my blood, the same as Killion. "What kind of cravings?"

She grew paler, more tufts sprouting here and there. "Things a shifter shouldn't want."

"The dead call to you?"

A grievous nod. Her lips trembled. "They frighten me."

"Join the club." I glanced at Andy. "What would you have me do?"

Andy placed a hand on her shoulder. "It was manageable until recently. Now it's getting worse for both her and her sister. We've tried various remedies but nothing works. I thought you might have an idea on how to help."

I didn't. They'd each only had a drop or two at most. "Aurora doesn't have a tea or concoction to null it, by chance?"

He shook his head. "She's mixed several potions. None have worked."

"And you're only telling me this now?"

"That's my fault," Pepper said, biting her bottom lip. "I was afraid you might...you know." She drew an invisible knife across her throat.

"You think I would harvest you because you've been infected by my blood?"

She dropped to a knee and threw her arms around my legs. "Please don't kill me!"

"Whoa." I patted the top of her head. "No one's dying today. I'm just not sure how to fix this."

She peered up at me with baleful eyes. "Can I stay here? With you?"

Extracting myself from her hold, I considered my options. "I'm not giving you more of my blood and I can't have you"—I waved a hand at her fur patches—"shifting in front of the humans. I'll talk to my boss. This can't be the first time this has happened in the history of grim reapers. Give me a day or so, okay?"

Her lips tightened but she nodded and stood. "Being close to you makes me feel better. Could I hang out right here? Just for a while?"

Guilt prickled under my skin. "Um, sure."

Relief cleared her eyes and she offered a tiny smile. The random tufts disappeared. "Being near enough to sense your presence is calming."

"Why don't you take her up to your apartment," I suggested to Andy. She might still be volatile and I didn't want her and the Tweedles to end up in a quarrel. Plus, this way I could telepathically speak to Killion about the situation and get his thoughts.

Andy shook his head. "No can do, amigo."

"Why not?"

"She's an unclaimed female. Doesn't matter that she's coyote and I'm wolf. Taking her into my home denotes a mating."

She made a face that matched his.

I had much to learn about the shifter clans and all their rules. "Unclaimed?"

"I haven't found a suitable mate," she said in defiance, "and I like my independence."

Andy held up his hands. "No judgment here. I would mate officially if I could, but since Aurora—" He glanced at me and stopped himself. "I'm just saying, inviting you into my home will cause us both problems."

Pepper sighed and nodded at me. "He's right. I'll stay here. It's no problem."

The weathered picnic table wasn't the most comfortable, and I still worried she and the vampires would eventually find each other intolerable. "We have a break room. Cramped but functional. Promise you'll stay put and not talk about supernatural things to my employees and you can hang out until my shift is over."

She threw herself at my legs again. "Thank you. I promise."

Andy smirked at my embarrassed grimace. "Please don't do that." I lifted her to her feet and instructed him to get her settled while I hailed the bodyguards. Andy and Pepper disappeared inside.

"I don't trust her," Cron mumbled to me when he resumed his station.

"Do you trust *any* shifter?"

"No," he snapped. "Neither should you."

I patted his ridiculously oversized bicep. "But I have

you and your twin here to protect me. What's there to worry about?"

He huffed and I winked before leaving the two of them to their guard duty.

Little did I realize Cron was right.

TEN

After handling a case of ear mites in Mr. Tennyson's cat, I caught up with Andy. He was in the kennel area trimming a Yorkie's nails and humming to himself. "Still here?" I asked, ruffling the dog's ears. She was focused on licking peanut butter off a silicone mat.

"Yep."

Unusual for him not to elaborate. "What did you mean earlier about you would mate if you could?"

"Nosy there, Grave Girl?"

Sensitive subject, apparently. I backed away, showing physical deference to his personal space. "Curiosity is my downfall."

He stopped mid-snip. "It's the one thing I can't fix."

"Aurora?"

A sharp nod and he returned to his task. "I knew it the moment I saw her. She's the one."

Was she the roadblock in the way of making their bond official, or was it some archaic pack rule? I wanted to press for details, but also needed to respect his privacy. "Is there anything I can do?"

He gave me a perplexed frown. "Unless you know how to change Aurora's mind about marriage, no."

"Marriage?" Andy hadn't struck me as the traditional type. And here, I'd assumed it was some pack thing, when in reality... "Have you proposed?"

"Three times and I'm considering it again on Valentine's Day."

"I had no idea." Why hadn't she told me? More importantly, why had she turned him down? "She's nuts about you, I know that. Maybe she's scared of commitment."

"I'm a wolf shifter. I'm not supposed to feel the call for a witch, and she's too independent to bind herself to someone." He shrugged. "It is what it is. After you harvested my soul and brought me back, I have a new perspective on life. I don't care about the pack rules or her thousand-and-one excuses. I love her and I don't want anybody else. She's my mate."

My heart did a quick *thudthud* in my chest, tugging on the thread that bound me to Killion. I suddenly wanted to see him, kiss him, feel his arms around me. "I totally get that. Don't give up."

Weak advice, but I wasn't much of a cheerleader. I filed the information away, determined to help if I could but knowing it wasn't my place to try and change my friend's mind.

After checking on Pepper, I wandered out back again, opening my connection to Killion. *I need you.*

Killion: *Rough day?*

Cron and Mags watched me with their intense dark eyes.

Me: *Just weird.* I gave him a brief rundown on everything that had transpired. *Any ideas on what I can do for the coyote?*

Killion: *Any effects of your blood should have worn off by now.*

Me: *They seem to be escalating.*

He was silent for a minute, thinking it over. *Give me twenty minutes. I'll wrap up my agenda and come straight away.*

Me: *You don't have to do that.* But I felt immense relief. I wanted to see him, like always. My touchstone in a crazy world.

Killion: *Of course, I do.* This was said with haughtiness and a bit of cheek. While I'd insisted on my independence, and the fact I didn't require anyone to save me, I did, in fact, want him. Our binding had created a partnership that went beyond anything I could describe—or deny.

We were equals, though. He needed me as much as I needed him, and we both knew it.

Me: *Careful with that tone or I'll make you pay for it later, vampire master.*

Killion: *I look forward to it.*

Again with the cheekiness. The connection ended, me grinning and shaking my head. The anticipation was delicious.

Neither guard met my eyes as I opened the door to return inside, but Cron had a smug smile.

I paused, studying him closely. "You weren't listening

to my conversation, were you? The master will make your Undead life miserable if you were."

Mags shot him a worried glance. Cron's smile faded. "I would never. I couldn't, even if I wanted to."

"Then what's with the smirk?"

His jaw clenched and he focused on a spot over my left shoulder.

"Spill or I'll torture you."

The tough guy act faltered ever so slightly. He huffed again, this time as a sigh. "You have tells when you speak to him."

Mags nodded. "I've noticed them, as well."

Annoyed, but curious, I moved back to look at both of them. "Like what?"

"Your scent changes," Mags volunteered. "And you smile a lot."

My scent? I sniffed inconspicuously, and yep, under the perfume of my soap and shampoo, layered with the clinic's distinct pet and cleaning product aromas, I was diffusing a healthy dose of pheromones into the air. Supes could smell them. I glanced at Cron. "Is that true?"

Forced to meet my gaze, he gave a cool, seemingly disinterested nod. "You touch your hair a lot, as well as your neck. I suggest you learn to control that. Any super-natural in range would know you're in contact with him."

Embarrassment heating my skin, I took another step back and tried to control my nervous heartbeat. He could probably hear it. "I'll take your counsel under advisement."

"They could manipulate you to draw him out, put him in danger," he added, as I reached for the knob.

Pausing, I wondered how, but shook my head. "No one is going to manipulate me and I certainly won't allow anyone to harm your master."

Neither said anything further. Smart vamps. I went back to work and Pepper did as instructed. When Patty asked about her, I said she was a college friend waiting for me to get off so we could go for drinks.

Killion arrived twenty minutes later on the dot. For privacy, we sat in his limo and he cloaked us so no one could hear our discussion. Ghost had gone crazy when she'd seen him arrive and now was in the front passenger seat, Moss making over her. His latest thing was teaching her tricks. She already knew how to sit and stay, but he'd upped the game and was teaching her to 'play dead' of all things.

"What's with all the secrecy?" I asked once I'd thoroughly kissed Killion. I climbed into his lap, and he ran his hands along my sides. "Did you want more than to discuss the coyote?"

He nipped at my bottom lip. "I always want more," he said, his voice a low rumble of need. "How much time do you have?"

Dr. O'Leary needed me in surgery in ten minutes. It wasn't our day for them, but like our earlier patient, the kitten who'd been found alongside the highway had a broken leg and couldn't wait. "Not long enough," I admitted.

We made out for a minute anyway, and then I forced myself to move off him. "Any ideas on what I should do?"

He tamed the locks of his hair that I'd mussed with my fingers. "You're not going to like it."

"There's nothing about this I do like. Hit me."

"Use compulsion to take away her craving."

"What? No way." I shook my finger at him. "You know how I feel about that."

"It is a temporary measure until we find a permanent solution, and you wouldn't be controlling her to do your will, only to relieve her symptoms. It would be a kindness."

I stewed. Logic won out again. "I don't know how."

"You can practice on me." He said it with a sly grin, taking the edge off my resistance. "Could be fun."

"You're doing that smoldering thing with your eyes."

The grin widened. "Is it working to bend you to my idea?"

Of course it was. "Manipulating anyone feels...I don't know...slimy."

"You would never use your power for evil. I'm confident you won't take advantage of me."

The last was said with a combination of self-confidence and challenge. I wasn't as confident, knowing Grim Zero could unleash hell on earth if provoked. I didn't want him to see my unease, however. "You sure about that, Fang Boy?"

He hated it when I called him that and reached over to tickle me. I gasped a laugh and knocked his hand away.

I wasn't excited about using compulsion on Pepper, but knowing that it was an option made me curious. Plus, practicing on Killion was safe. He would never let me take advantage of him. "How exactly do I do it?"

"Open your faucet and send my arm a silent command. Make me raise it."

The faucet analogy had worked for me when it came to allowing my magic to flow. I closed my eyes and sent a trickle into the mental channel between us. *Lift.*

The command was more a suggestion, and it slid like sticky pudding between us, rather than flowing with the ease of water.

"You're resisting," Killion said. "Relax. Think of it as fun."

I could think of other things than forcing him to raise his arm in the air that qualified as such. *Kiss me.*

The floodgates of my magic flung wide and the next thing I knew I was once more in his lap with his lips on mine.

Everything exploded inside me. Talk about compulsion—it felt as if I'd done it to myself.

"You did," he confirmed, dragging his lips from mine to kiss my jaw, my neck. "It boomeranged."

Like so many other things with us now. I laughed. "Good to know." It was a type of relief. "I can't force you to do anything without forcing myself to do it, too."

"That should keep your evil plans for me in check."

I smacked him playfully, knowing his teasing carried a bit of truth. I'd made friends with Grim Zero, but it felt fragile and tenuous. My alter ego, as I thought of her, could conceivably change the world, and not for the better.

Forcing a grin, I pretended not to let that idea, always hovering over me, show in my eyes. "And yours for me, as well."

He massaged the back of my neck. "Perhaps we should practice more tonight."

I kissed him deeply. "I can hardly wait."

Breathless as I reluctantly climbed out, I turned when he called, "You can ask her permission, you know."

True. I could simply explain to Pepper that it would help. Being a shifter, and me yoked to a vampire, she would probably hate it, but it might still be worth pursuing.

Ghost whined but stayed planted in the front with Moss. I nodded at Killion, ruffled her fur, and told the driver to take care of her for me. He promised to teach her more tricks and I waved the lot of them off, the promise of a night of 'fun' in Killion's violet eyes.

Nita met me on the sidewalk. "There you are." She was dressed in a peach raincoat with matching slip ons with bows. Her eyeliner was thick and her hair in a cute updo that looked casual and breezy, but I'd never be able to pull it off. She watched the limo gliding out of sight.

"You're up and about."

"I took a megadose of pain killers with an energy drink and it worked to get rid of the migraine." Her gaze trailed after the limo. "What did you get tall, dark, and mysterious for Valentine's Day?"

"Ugh, I hate this holiday. Nothing."

She pointed to the clinic windows decorated with shiny hearts and cupids. The work of Megan, my part-time teenage assistant, who was fixated with death but also crushing on Mason. About ten of Cupid's arrows had hit her. "But it's the day for lovers. Please don't tell me you forgot, Morticia."

She rarely called me the pet nickname these days,

since I'd found a replacement for my position at the morgue. "I didn't forget. I just..."

Sighing like a heavyweight champion forced to train a novice, she put an arm around my shoulders and walked me inside. "You know he's getting you something amazing. Expensive. Something to knock your mismatched socks off. That's how he is."

Patty greeted her as I glanced down at my feet. I hadn't even noticed I was wearing one pink and one green.

"Knowing him, he's probably planned a whole romantic getaway." Her sigh this time was dreamy. "You totally deserve it, but I don't know how you got so lucky."

I doubted there was any vacation in my future with all the SMG directives on my plate, although I had mentioned that I wanted to see his homeland someday, along with the castle I'd seen when I'd touched his family ring once that had triggered a vision of the past. He still held ownership of the place, although only a couple of servants lived there to keep it up. "What should I get him?"

"Tough one." Several clients in the waiting area were acting like they weren't eavesdropping. It was hard not to in the cramped space, and normally, I would have ushered her to the break room, but Pepper was there. "I mean, he's rich and has everything he could want." She shrugged.

"He doesn't want *stuff*," Patty chimed in. "All he wants is you, Chloe. Give him something from your heart. Make a gesture to show you care about the same things he does."

Nita elbowed me and winked. "A gesture with satin and lace, perhaps?" Her voice dropped to a conspiratorial whispered, "Or leather and chains?"

I dragged her behind the desk, smiling at the waiting pet owners and praying none had heard that. "*Not helpful*," I muttered to her.

"We could dye your streak again." Now Patty winked.

That actually was a good idea for several reasons. I liked matching Killion's eye color and it made me look young, rather than older. It was cool having an office manager who did hair on the side. "Definitely."

Patty wrote on her calendar. "Wednesday after you're done here. I'll bring my supplies."

"And we can go shopping," Nita suggested. "We haven't hung out in weeks, and you need something new for Darcy's party."

"What party?"

JR, my grade school friend turned veterinarian, interrupted, dropping a file on Patty's desk. "Hey, Nita." He was sharp in his slacks and button down, his lab coat lending an air of authority. It was open, keeping him casual and dashing.

Nita looked him over. "Hello, doctor."

He returned her smile, his attention dropping to her lips. "You're not stealing my favorite tech away, now are you?"

She threw an arm around my shoulder. "I would if I could. We were discussing plans to go to a Valentine's party. Morticia, here, needs a new dress."

"No dresses," I said. "I don't remember anything about this get-together."

She forced me to face her, hanging onto my shoulders. "You promised!"

"I did?" I'm far from being a social butterfly, and I'm not a fan of Darcy's. "I'm pretty sure I have plans that night."

"Ugh." She released me and spun to JR. "Do you see what I'm dealing with? She's going to ghost me. There I'll be without backup."

"*Ghost*," Corvus mimicked. "Kill."

All eyes turned to him in the window on his perch.

"If you need a wingman..." JR was used to the talking bird and let the words trail off. I simply took a step back, shaking my head at what was happening. Watching with an equal amount of interest, Patty winked at me. "I mean, I wouldn't want to impose, or anything, but I'm not one to leave a friend stranded. We have to stick together."

Nita gave me a reproachful eye. "Exactly. At least somebody gets it."

"Chloe?" Dr. O'Leary stood at the end the hall ready to go.

"Coming," I called. "Catch you later, Gomez," I said to Nita. "I promise to text later, okay?"

She barely acknowledged my exit, too busy giving JR the party details to notice.

ELEVEN

The rest of my afternoon went by in a haze of pet hair, being peed on by an iguana, and consternation over what to get Killion for a gift. The kitten's surgery went smoothly and Vera agreed to foster him until he was well enough to be adopted.

Patty was teaching Corvus new words, as well as addressing his manners, and offered to take him home with her that night. She missed her raven and he filled that void. It was with some relief that I agreed.

Twice I bolstered my courage to use compulsion on Pepper, and twice I chickened out. She was so quiet and patient, staying in the break room the whole time without complaint that at one point I forgot she was there until she asked permission to use the restroom. It was only then when the situation truly sank home—I had become her alpha, whether I wanted to be or not.

When she returned, I had a cup of Aurora's tea waiting for her. "Have a seat."

She did, sniffing the herbal brew. "Smells like chai."

"It is." With an extra kick of magic. "You've been incredibly patient and I appreciate it."

"Did you figure out what we should do?"

"Yes."

"Really?" Maybe it was the overhead lighting, but her eyes appeared to flash as she sipped. It was there and gone as fast as lightning. Surprise, curiosity, doubt. She blinked and did a double take at the cup of liquid. Her body swayed ever so slightly. "You...spelled...the tea?"

I touched her arm, making contact as I lightly brushed the bioelectricity of her brain with mine. "I'm not a witch," I told her, praying the tiny bit of compulsion I sent into the herbs would calm any fears she had. "And I'm not so much worried about your desire to serve me, although that's definitely a no-go, as I am about the dead calling to you. I know how harrowing that can be."

As she stared into my eyes, they mesmerized her and she visibly relaxed. "Yes."

"We can't have you terrified of them, or feeling the need to raise them." I kept my voice steady, gentle. "I'm blocking them from you. You no longer sense them." There was no resistance in her mind. The strange thing was, I couldn't find any calling card of my blood in her body. I had expected at least some. "You are not bound to me in any manner, nor subservient. You are free from any connection tasting my blood created."

"I'm free from you."

"That's correct." I focused on pulling my magic away now like an ebbing tide. "You can return to your normal life, okay?"

She bobbed her head. "Okay."

Removing my touch, I cut off the connection and sat back in the chair, exhausted and exhilarated at the same time.

She blinked a few times, shoved the cup aside and stood. "Is that it?"

"How do you feel?"

A shoulder lifted and fell in unconcerned nonchalance. "Fine." She glanced toward the exit and shifted her weight back and forth. "Thanks."

The earlier friendliness and idol worship was definitely gone. I was relieved, but something felt off. "I'll give you a ride home, just let me grab my stuff."

I made the rounds to lock up and turn off the lights. Tapping into my telepathic connection to Killion, I felt buoyed. *I did it my way,* I told him, *and I think it worked.*

Killion: *Very good. I'm wrapping up here. I'll see you for dinner.*

Me: *Be naked when I get there. I want to play with your dragon.*

Killion: *Dangerous game, that.*

Me, grinning: *I live for danger.*

I heard his chuckle. *As you wish.*

I checked on the kitten, and found her sleeping. We had an older female cat nearly recovered from a bad case of ear mites and she'd taken to her. I'd placed them in a kennel reserved for large dogs. Andy would check on them during the evening.

I was speaking softly to the newly anointed momma when I heard the back door squeak and the sound of voices. The cat backed from my hand and hissed.

Cron and Mags, no doubt. I rolled my eyes. "Don't worry, I'll get them out of here."

It wasn't the bodyguards waiting for me, however.

Lasarus and two of his vampires, including the female I'd seen in the bar the previous night, filled the space and blocked the exit. The male was holding Pepper hostage.

"Lord Killion's playmate." Lasarus sniffed the air as he stalked me, edging around me in a circle. "I could smell you all over him last night."

Lord Killion?

"He always did have a weakness for humans," the female vamp rasped. She checked me over from head to toe, clicking her tongue. "Though you are rather plain for his tastes."

"Rude, much?" I sent a pulse of magic out as a warning, and all three vamps paused, reassessing me.

"We know you're a grim," Lasarus said, unconcerned. In fact, he seemed almost eager to engage me. "We also know by SMG's code that you cannot harvest us if our contracts aren't up."

The bodyguards had to be dead. *My fault, my fault, my fault.* Killion was right to worry about security. And where was that magic suppressing belt when I needed it? I'd left it at the penthouse.

I forced a smile. "Lucky for me, there's always an exception, especially since my boss absolutely hates the Undead. Since you're already on SMG's radar for killing three people, they'll consider reaping you a service to humanity."

"Three?" Lasarus laughed, a cold, calculating sound

that raised the hairs on the back of my neck. "I've taken far more than that. How many do you have under your robes, reaper?"

Was he baiting me? I didn't have my scythe nor my psychopomp. Technically, I needed at least one to reap them. However, being Grim Zero had its benefits. If I could get close enough to place my hand over his heart, next to the spot where his soul had once resided, I could still end him. I'd done it before.

"You said if I did what you wanted, you'd let me go," Pepper whined.

"You betrayed me." Even as I said it, things made more sense. She wasn't having side effects from my blood —that had been a ruse. She'd waited so patiently because she'd been spying on me, looking for the opportune moment to let them know when I was alone and vulnerable. I'd truly believed she felt bound to me. "Well played." Her brown eyes flickered with regret but I didn't care. "If they let you go, and they won't, you have a new enemy to worry about."

"He said he'd kill my sister."

Of course, he had. I met the leader's black eyes. "He still will. Unless I stop him."

He smirked. "How do you think you'll do that? There's nobody here to rescue you and you're no match for the three of us."

"You're right, except for one small detail."

The smirk grew. "Oh, yeah? And what's—"

I lifted the table and hit him with it before he finished. "I don't need rescuing." The wood splintered, the teacup sailing through the air and smacking his female friend. "Shift!" I yelled at Pepper.

My grim strength and speed alone might not have been a match for the strigoi, but my bond to Killion increased them tenfold. I flowed through the fight like a well-oiled machine, not thinking, but opening the channel of my power to its max.

A table leg became a weapon; Pepper, now a coyote, a tool. Under the circumstances, I didn't have qualms about using compulsion on her. I easily accessed her animal nature, pushing her fighting instincts to a higher and more dangerous level.

They were still formidable opponents. The female lashed at me with long nails and undid the chain belt around her waist to strike at the wood stake in my hand. Lasarus, taking a page from my playbook, armed himself with two other table legs, while his male companion used a chair to fend off Pepper in animal form like a lion tamer at the circus.

Pushing a wave of magic at them, it had the desired effect of a moment's distraction. Instead of continuing the battle with Lasarus and his partner, I ducked under their assaults and turned on the second male and Pepper. Ripping the chair from his grasp, the shocked strigoi stumbled back, crashing into the counter behind him. "Kill," I ordered the coyote.

She leaped, taking him to the floor, jaws around his neck. A cry of fear mixed with pain erupted before it turned to a gurgle.

"You bitch," the female spat. She lunged.

"She's mine, Sable," Lasarus growled. He flowed so

quickly I couldn't follow the movement and smacked the back of my head with a blow that rattled my teeth. The room swam for a blink but I laughed and swerved out of the way of the follow-up blow. The chain belt struck my thigh, cutting through my pants and shredding skin, but it was now two against two. I liked those odds better.

Neither moved to stop the coyote from ripping out their friend's throat. I took a step toward her, smiling at them and using a feeler of magic to search for their most vulnerable weakness. I couldn't immediately sense any, yet knew each had to have one.

Their nostrils flared at the coppery tang of blood and Lasarus grinned back, springing at me. At the same instant, his companion went for Pepper.

That was his weakness—he was too confident. He had no patience and believed himself the alpha in the room.

Time to depose him of that idea.

Growls, snarls, yips, and my war cries filled the space as the four of us fought. Blood and fur flew. Lasarus went for my neck with a beefy hand and sank his nails into the tendons there, putting pressure on my windpipe.

I let him.

Thinking he was, indeed, the top dog in this scenario, he gave a triumphant laugh as he lifted me into the air. My feet swung free and I gurgled, trying to breathe. "You're mine, reaper. You'll do what I say."

The lack of oxygen made me lightheaded, but I only faked being helpless. His companion let out a cry of pain as Pepper sank her teeth deep into the woman's thigh. Lasarus didn't take his eyes off me, and I let mine drift shut. *One..., two..., three...* I counted off the seconds and then I caught the strigoi where I knew it would hurt the most.

I'd never played football, never kicked a field goal, but I swung my leg for all I was worth. Even with the lack of air in my lungs, my strength was still superhuman and when my foot connected with his groin, he yelped, dropped me, and doubled over.

Crumpling to the floor, I dragged in a huge breath. Thanks to Katarina's training, I knew to keep him down and kicked out again, this time catching him in the face. His nose broke and blood streamed from it as he hollered, grabbing his crotch and face simultaneously.

Pepper and Sable continued to tussle and my quick reflexes helped the coyote when I tripped Sable. She went down and bounced back up, snarling at me.

"One second," I told her, holding up a finger. "I have to take care of your leader first."

I bent and placed my hand on Lasarus' chest. The place where his soul should reside was but a blank, hollow expanse. His heart didn't beat, but I felt the flow of blood in his veins.

He swung at me, knocking me away and I cold-cocked him upside the head. He swore in some old, forgotten language, his eyes buggy as he blinked and tried to stay conscious. Fiery pain tore through my fist and up my arm.

I grabbed a chunk of his hair and banged his head on the floor hard enough to make him bark. When his companion raked her nails down my back, I reached behind me lightning quick and pushed her sideways.

The scratches hurt and she'd torn one of my favorite blouses. Was there magic to fix it? I'd have to ask Pennyworth.

Reaching for Lasarus again, I smacked my palm onto his chest. "Hold still. This will be over in the beat of your heart."

The organ did, in fact, beat as I tugged at his soul to return to his body so I could harvest it. The technicalities of the broken contracts vampires had with Death and SMG were beyond me, but I knew how to raise the dead —and the Undead—in order to reap them permanently.

"*Enough.*"

The presence of the angel himself, as well as his stern command, sliced through me like a hot knife. Death.

"I've got it," I growled.

"Let him go."

Whipping my head around to look at the six-seven figure looming over me, I panted. "What? Why?"

"We have important things to attend to." He reached down and pulled me off the strigoi. Then he said to Lasarus and Sable, "Get out. Don't bother the grim again."

The two scrambled for the exit, both bleeding. They stumbled over their dead companion without hesitation and left the door open as they fled. Pepper backed her coyote self into a corner, looking like she was going to be sick.

"Go home to your sister and stay out of trouble," Death said, pointing outside. "Chloe will be in touch."

She bolted and I jerked my arm from his grasp. "You just ruined my fun and let those killers go free."

"If you'd completed the job required of you, this might not have happened."

"But—"

He held up a hand, every ounce of patience absent from his glare. "Enough."

"You're an idiot." I raced to the alley to check on Con and Mags. They lay on the ground, eyes clouded with pain, mouths contorted in silent screams. Wooden stakes pierced their chests and they seemed...less there. As if they were shrinking. "You couldn't have intervened a few minutes sooner and saved them?" I called.

Death stood at the top of the steps. "They aren't my concern."

I grunted as I tugged at the stakes. They were definitely in deep. Sweating, I tossed each to the ground, watching the vampires for any sign of life.

Death stood in the doorway. "We need to go."

"I still don't understand why you let Lasarus and Sable get away."

"While they're guilty of plenty of crimes, and I'd enjoy their mutual demise, they may be useful down the road. Come on." He motioned me to come back inside the clinic.

Chloe?

It was Killion. Me: *I'm okay. Lasarus got away. Your bodyguards are down. Death is acting weird.*

Killion: *I'm almost there. Stay put.*

Unfortunately, I didn't get to, nor did I get to say anything else. The moment I crossed the threshold, Death took me for a ride.

TWELVE

Thanks to Death, I went from the clinic to a colossal hall made of marble pillars, towering archways, and a ceiling so far above my head I could barely see it. It disappeared into bright blue sky with pillow clouds.

The moment my feet touched the stone floor, my stomach pitched and I staggered as if drunk. Slamming into a pillar, I bent over, grabbing my rolling stomach.

"Do not vomit in the Hall of Souls," he growled. His usual Australian accent was barely detectable and he was dressed impeccably in gray slacks and a white shirt. Even his shoulder-length hair was groomed and combed back. "Mei doesn't take well to outsiders desecrating her sacred space."

Mimicking him under my breath like a teenager annoyed with a parent, I straightened, gazing at the never ending hall and soaring windows. A glance out one showed an azure sky over a mountain range. "Is this heaven?"

"No." He started walking and I pushed off the marble and hurried to catch up. "If I send Tinder to bring you in, you come. Are we clear?"

Every archway led to a wing of more expansive halls. I watched a few people milling around but any who saw us—or rather, the scowling thundercloud beside me—turned and ran in the other direction.

I used my telepathy to reach out to Killion but grimaced at the static that filled my head. A cold apprehension wound around my chest. "We have to go back. I didn't lock up and Killion will be worried."

"The vampire will be fine." Death took a left and I practically had to jog to keep up with him. "Take care of the ghost and you can return."

I hated being bossed around. Too bad I couldn't use compulsion on my boss. "This spirit must be quite the annoyance if you and the Mighty Oz can't handle it."

His eyes slid to me. "Who?"

"Mei Han? The short guy behind the curtain?"

"Your movie references get tiresome after a while."

"Well, you have a thing for being a pain in my a—"

"Chloe." The woman in question appeared out of nowhere, startling me and bringing us both to a dead stop. Her midnight black hair was its usual straight self, complete with bangs, and her guarded gaze stared at me from behind thick-rimmed glasses. "It's about time."

"We were on our way to your office," Death said with none of the irritation in his voice that he'd spoken to me with. "I apologize for the delay."

Mei's harsh black pantsuit matched her straight hair.

"Urgency has never been your strong suit. Take care of the problem. I'll be back momentarily."

She marched off, leaving me gaping at her petite figure as it disappeared into nothingness. My chest ached and I rubbed at the area around my heart. I caught myself reaching for Killion's presence. Like a phantom limb, my body expected him to be there, but he wasn't. "Let's get this over with so I can go home."

A dog's bark echoed through the space, bouncing off the marble and stone. I knew that sound. "Ghost?"

Sure enough, my psychopomp came into view from the opposite direction, running full tilt at me. I bent and she leaped into my arms, licking my chin. "I thought you were learning more tricks with Moss." Despite the situation, I laughed at her enthusiasm. "Guess you got shanghaied like me, huh?"

"You'll need her to take the spirit to the afterlife."

I glanced up to find Death still sporting the latest in stormy couture. I got to my feet, lifting Ghost with me. "What *is* your problem? I thought we'd gotten past your pissy-ness over my bonding with Killion."

His chest heaved and he glared at me with a look that made my insides shudder. "This has nothing to do with you or that piece of worthless—"

"Say one more snide thing about him and I'll make sure your ghost haunts this place forever."

"It's not all about you, you know." My scythe appeared in his massive hands and he shoved it at me. "Once in an eon you might take a break from The Chloe Show and think about others."

What? That was a low blow and he knew it. I was

constantly putting those I cared about before my own wants and needs.

"Is this goad Chloe day?" I snatched the blade from him. "Are you having a breakdown or something? You're always irascible but this is extreme, even for you."

He turned and waved a hand at the towering golden doors in front of us. I hadn't even noticed them, their tops disappearing into the sky far above. As they began to open, a slit of icy blue light cut through them, nearly blinding me. I flinched, raising the hand with the weapon to block its intensity.

As the opening yawned larger, a wave of frigid air swept over me. Without moving my feet, I was drawn inside as if I were on an invisible moving platform. More of Death's magic? Or Mei's?

Crisp air filled my nose. I blinked to help my eyes adjust, but felt dizzy when I took in her office. Ghost whined low in her throat. We were no longer standing on a marble floor—we were on the precipice of a mountain.

"Holy reapers." If I reached out, I was sure I could touch a cloud floating by. Turning slowly in a circle, snow crunched under my shoes. The view in every direction was nothing but more ragged mountain tops and deep valleys that I couldn't see the bottom of. In front of us, the desk I had seen in the hologram meeting presided in the air. "This is an impressive illusion."

Death, next to me, crossed his arms over his massive chest. "It's no illusion. Find the ghost, cross him over, and you can go back to your precious vampire."

I waved the scythe in front of me at the endless peaks and valleys. There was no end to them. "Here? *Where?*"

Death slapped me on the back and strode for the doors. "I'll be by later to check on you."

"Wait!" He didn't, those golden doors slamming shut behind him. I cursed, shuffling through the snow to them. Setting Ghost down, I gave them a shove.

They didn't budge. I tried slamming some of my magic into them, but it felt dull in my chest and didn't faze them in the least. I mentally called to Killion again, static once more filling my ears.

"I hate you," I yelled.

Ghost sniffed at a leg of the floating desk. Leaning against the massive doors, I once more surveyed the 'office.' "I don't care if you pee on that, just don't fall off the edge."

How was I supposed to find a ghost in this maze of a landscape that stretched as far as I could see? It wasn't like I could simply ask the spirit to come talk to me.

Or could I?

"Hello?" My voice echoed over the summit and down into the valley. *Helloo...hellooo...hellooooo.* "My name is Chloe. I know Mei isn't much of a conversationalist. Would you like to talk to me?"

Nothing happened. I strolled to the desk and eyed the piles of blue folders that matched the color of the sky. As long as I was here, what did it hurt to be nosy and see what the head of Soul Management Group was up to? "I'm just over here hanging out," I continued, my voice flowing over the landscape. "I'm happy to chat if you want."

Ghost pawed my leg and I pointed at the chair. She hopped right up and made herself comfortable.

The first folder I touched zapped me so hard it knocked me on my butt and sent me sliding along the icy ground. I grappled for something to stop me as the ledge loomed. "Ack!"

My scythe bumped over the frozen ground and I nearly slid off, but managed to hook it into a crevice. My feet kept sliding, however, taking my lower half with them.

I screamed as they went over the edge. Ghost leaped from the seat and morphed, even as my grip on the blade jerked me to a stop. Hanging suspended in the air, I choked and tried to call for help, but my voice came out a sob.

Not daring to look down at the miles and miles of rocky mountainside, I swung my free arm up and grasped at the scythe handle. Ghost sank her giant canines into my arm and I cried out again, this time in pain, but was grateful when she hauled me up.

Heart racing, I eased from the overhang, swallowing the fear pulsing in my throat, as I slid away from the ledge.

She nuzzled my face and I released my white-knuckle grip on the blade to hug her. "Thanks," I murmured into her fur. She licked my cheek.

Gaining my feet, I brushed snow from my pants and watched as the blood dripping from her bite disappeared into the snow. "I will pay you back for that," I promised Mei.

Ghost remained in psychopomp form. I gingerly pulled out the chair, and when I didn't get a similar jolt, sat. Drawing a ragged breath, I slowly swiveled around, scanning the horizon. Surprisingly, the seat didn't seem to be spelled with any repelling magic, so I kicked my feet up on the desk and knocked Mei's neat pile of folders over with great satisfaction. "Oops," I chuckled.

Crystals of ice and snow fell on her blotter, instantly evaporating without damaging anything.

Focus, Chloe. It was time to get this over with so we could go home. I would deal with Mei later. "Come out, come out, whoever you are. I don't blame you for haunting this place out of spite, but is it worth it?" I shivered in the chilly air and rubbed my arms. Death could've at least warned me I would need a coat.

When no spectral appeared, I dropped my feet back to the ground and stomped them. "I can think of nicer places to hang," I shouted, again listening to the echo. "I can't imagine spending eternity with the sourpuss who runs this place."

Another cloud floated by, and as my words died off in the distance, I realized how eerily quiet it was. My stomach growled, and even that seemed to echo over the land. Killion had to be freaking out big time. I certainly was.

I tapped into my magic, digging deep. It felt dull and lifeless, like something was smothering it. Had to be the magic in this place, but I didn't know how to break free from it.

Ghost nudged me with her nose. I frowned at her pleading eyes. "You're *not* going to run off and explore. I know it's tempting. We need to find this ghost and get out of here. Suggestions?"

She tilted her head up and howled.

The sound reverberated through me and over the snow caps. A rumbling started under my feet. The echo went on and on and on, seeming to grow louder, rather than fading. I had to cover my ears.

Across the expanse, it seemed to cause the distant peaks to quake. "Uh oh."

What started as one became a cascade of avalanches. The sky overhead went gray, the wispy clouds turning into thunderheads.

"Not good," I said, raising my voice over the building resonance. Even my bones quaked.

I grabbed the scythe with one hand and her scruff with the other. The ground beneath us fissured, the crevice I'd anchored my blade in spreading wide and coming right for us.

I ran, dragging Ghost to the doors. while the desk continued to float above the earthquake-damaged ground. The chair disappeared into the growing gap.

"Can you get us out of here?" I cried.

Her liquid eyes turned to me, and, as the ground gave out under us, I swear she grinned.

THIRTEEN

We landed in the living room of Killion's suite, me on my head after tumbling over an end table and taking out a new lamp. The expensive piece flew high into the air and promptly came down on my face.

"Ow!" I batted it aside, blinking back tears from the smack on the nose. Gingerly, I tested the cartilage and squeaked again. Was it broken?

At least the lamp was intact. Hopefully, it was still in working condition.

Inter-dimensional travel always made me sick to my stomach. I opened the link to Killion, and it was fuzzy, but I sent out a message. *At your place. Death will be coming for me. Hurry.*

When Ghost growled viciously, I shifted, rolling to my hands and knees, but I swayed as the room seemed to dip.

Killion: *Are you okay? Where have you been?*

Seeing double, I held down my stomach contents, and blinked to clear my vision. The lamp had been yanked from the socket and the room darkening shades were drawn. I couldn't even see my throbbing nose.

Me: *SMG. I had no choice.*

Killion: *Did you cross their ghost?*

Me: *More like wrecked Mei's office.*

A chuckle. *Be there shortly.*

With my head swimming, I grasped the sofa arm and hauled myself to my feet, my neck and shoulders rippling with pain.

At least I hadn't ended up at the bottom of Mei's mountains.

"What is it, girl?" I asked the dog, feeling around for my scythe. The normal scent of Killion's warm caramel and old libraries magic was absent, but I couldn't pick up any aromas, not even those of the butler's good cooking. Probably because my nose was swelling. "Pennyworth? Are you here?"

"Yes." His voice came from across the room and was strained, as if his tie were choking him. "You shouldn't have come."

"Shut up," someone said.

Goosebumps rose on my arms. I knew that voice. "What are you doing here?" Where was that scythe? I picked up the heavy lamp instead and cocked it, ready to strike. If only I could see. "How did you get in?"

The overhead light flared to life, casting a soft glow on the room that still managed to blind me temporarily. I blinked again. *Come on eyes, adjust!*

I froze at the sight of Lasarus with an arm around

Pennyworth's neck. He had a wooden stake aimed at the vamp's heart, the sharp tip pricking the butler's shirt. "I have endless resources and friends with amazing talents."

I lowered the lamp. My scythe was trapped under Sable's foot. She gave me a blasé grin, picking at her nails. Ghost, still in psychopomp form, sidled up next to me. I opened the channel to Killion before I replied. "What do you want?"

"I think you know the answer to that." Lasarus pressed the stake harder into Pennyworth's chest, making an indentation in the silk shirt. The Undead butler, and best cook in Louisiana—don't tell my aunt—flinched, eyes widening.

Killion roared in my head. *What is he doing there?*

Threatening my favorite house elf. Don't worry, I've got this. With the heavy wards on this place, there was no way he and his girlfriend should have been able to get in. What *friend* had helped him? "Release the butler."

"You know what I want." He smiled. It was cold and brutal, centuries of honed blood thirst and ruthlessness wrapped up in it.

Not letting the icy fear for Pennyworth's life settle into my bones, I righted the table and set the lamp on it, trying to act as unconcerned as they appeared. I itched to send out a wave of magic to alert the entire hotel staff, but if they came busting in without realizing the situation, the butler could end up staked. I warned Killion in case he was considering the same. "Here's the thing—we don't always get what we want."

Sable snarled. Ghost did, too. I stood, continuing to act calm while Lasarus eyed me with speculation. "You don't have your boss here to protect you this time," he said with a glint in his soulless eyes. "And your master isn't here, either."

"Death will be here soon." If nothing else, he'd be livid over the destruction of Mei's office and be on the hunt to bring me back to SMG. "And trust me, he's not in a good mood. You won't get a second chance with him. As far as Killion goes, he's not my master, and I don't need him to resolve this situation. It's just you and me." I ignored Sable's grunt of annoyance at being ignored. "You seem to believe that's a problem for me, but let me assure you, you're in more danger than I am."

She picked up the scythe and I heard its siren song in my head. *Kill.* She tapped the blade in her palm. "We'll be ready for Death, and I'm so going to enjoy making you suffer."

"I'm not sure you can be *ready* for Death. He's, well, *death.* You do realize you can't kill him, even with that weapon."

Her sneer turned wolfish. "I'm certainly willing to give it a try."

Plenty of entities had through the ages.

I shrugged, forcing myself to stay relaxed. No way I was allowing either of them to sense, hear, or smell my fear. "Okay then. Good luck with that. Meantime,"—I pointed to Lasarus and Pennyworth—"I'll go with you peacefully if you release him."

"You're a fool." The strigoi lowered the stake and shoved the butler away. Pennyworth toppled to the new rug near the hearth and stayed down, but sent me a warning look. "You seem to have no concern for yourself, always saving others."

He obviously hadn't chatted with my boss about The Chloe Show.

If only I had that magic suppressing belt! I couldn't fathom why he'd so easily given up but it was the opportune time to use it on him. "I may be a fool, but it seems you're an idiot."

He flipped the stake end over end, the corners of his mouth quirking in a vicious smile. "Is that so?"

Before I could react, he threw it at my heart.

I staggered at the impact, the sheer shock of it overriding the searing agony as the sharpened tip pierced my chest with frightening ease. "Did not see that...coming." I fell to my knees.

A raging Ghost leaped into the air, her fierce barking and snarling echoing in my ears. He caught her as her body slammed into his, the two of them crashing into the floor-to-ceiling bookshelf behind them.

"Chloe!" Pennyworth's cry snapped my attention to him, blood seeping through my shirt. *Too much.* It was flowing like a river.

Kill, I heard the scythe croon.

"Look out!" The butler pushed up and pointed.

Catching the glint of metal from the corner of my eye, I twisted in time to see Sable raising the weapon over my head.

She wasn't after Death—she was after me.

I raised an arm to ward off the blow, but the world tilted. As the blade cleaved the air with a melodic zing,

Pennyworth launched himself from his place and threw himself in front of it.

"*No*," I screamed.

The steel cut through his neck with a sickening sound. As I gasped, his head thunked to the floor and rolled past me.

FOURTEEN

Fury roared out of me and I loosed a wordless cry. The power of my magic knocked Ghost, Lasarus, and Sable off their feet. Ghost, wild in her own wrath, pounced on top of the strigoi leader, pinning him under her.

I crawled to Pennyworth's body, sobbing.

There was nothing I could do. A fiery sensation spread through my veins as my heart struggled to pump. Blood continued to pour from the wound in my chest, dripping all over him.

The door flew open behind me. "You're dead," I heard Killion snarl with ice-filled malice. *"You're both dead."*

He moved too quickly for me to track, my lungs constricting. I started to tug the stake free, but Katarina and Aurora were suddenly on either side of me, Katarina knocking my shaking fingers away. "Leave it."

Hands went under my armpits, lifting me and

carrying me from the living room. Ghost and Killion fought with the two strigoi, a wolf joining in—Andy.

"I have to..." The world went sideways again as Katarina laid me on the long dining table. The thought fled my brain; all I could remember was Pennyworth's eyes right before...

No. I shoved her hands aside and tried to rise. My body howled in pain from the movement. I tumbled to the floor, whimpering.

My vision went dark. I could hear the fight raging in the other room, and I tried to crawl toward them. I would not let Lasarus escape. I had to find some way to help the butler. I had to...

My body twitched, the stake trembling with it. Agony tore through my limbs, seeming to shred muscle and tendons, a raging fire in my veins. Froth formed at the corners of my mouth.

The stake. My heart. *Killion.*

If it was affecting me like this, was it also hurting him?

That was the plan, wasn't it? I'd been wrong again. Lasarus and Sable weren't after me or Pennyworth. They wanted Killion.

I was yanked from the floor, my vision clearing enough to see the ceiling as my back hit the table. Katarina came into view and glared down at me. "You've been poisoned. Stay still. The more you struggle the more it will spread."

Aurora's voice was panicked. "What type?" I heard the rattle of glass vials. "I can put together an antidote."

In the background, I heard Ghost yelp and Sable

laugh. It was cut short and I felt the clashing of magics skitter over my skin as Killion and Andy fought her and Lasarus. Time seemed to spin out. I suddenly couldn't remember why they were fighting, why my body hurt so badly, why I couldn't seem to breathe.

I coughed and blood spurted from me into Katarina's face. She froze and backed away, hissing. "Sorry. I can't... breathe..." I coughed and sputtered again.

The sound of glass breaking, Andy howling, Ghost snarling, and then silence. Eerie and heart-rendering silence, as if my ears were in a vacuum.

I blinked, trying to stay conscious, my limbs twitched and jerked, the fire raging higher and blotting out everything. My heart beat stuttered. The darkness closed in.

Far away, I heard Aurora crying. "No, no, no. Fight it, Chloe!"

I tried to tell her it was okay, that I would be back. I couldn't remember why I thought that, and then I heard Killion's demand, "Chloe, I'm here. Don't leave me."

I felt his hands on my body. His magic coursing through me, chasing the poison, suffocating it.

My magic surged, reaching for him. I blinked back the darkness, swallowed against the vacuum. The room swam into view, the hovering faces over me blurry, but there. "Is Ghost...?"

He caressed my brow. "She will be fine. As will you." His voice was strained. I felt his agony, a rebound of my own. "The strigoi are gone and I must remove the stake, or—"

"You can't," Aurora interrupted. "She'll bleed out."

"And if he doesn't," Katarina said, "they'll both die."

My heart stuttered again, my breath nothing but a sharp, agonizing gasp. With the last of my energy, I reached up and yanked the poisoned wood out myself.

Relief.

"What the...?" Death's booming voice made me flinch. He shoved the others away, even Killion, and I was lifted once more, this time with gentleness. "Move, vampire, or I'll end your sorry life myself."

"She's dying," Killion barked. His voice shook, pain, grief, anger intertwined in the words. "Save her."

"She's already dead." I felt the brush of wings. Death's feathers. My heart had indeed stopped. "Now get out of my way and let me have her."

Inside the void of the in-between, my spirit hovered. I'd been here before, although I didn't remember the first few times. How many more did I have left? Didn't matter. I had to leave before my death caused Killion's. I had to escape this Land of the Dead—neither heaven, nor hell, but definitely not for me.

All was peace, the burning and suffering gone. I didn't need oxygen, didn't need anything. I floated, nothing more than a feather in the ancient wings of Death.

A pinprick of light flickered, snagging my consciousness. I felt a tug where my breastbone was. A thread that called me to Killion through time and space. *I'm coming...*

The hum of words buzzed my inner ear. Other spirits were caught here.

"Chloe?" It was Pennyworth. His ghost appeared,

glancing around at the darkness that was both inside me and not. "What happened?"

It was so good to see him, I felt my eyes fill with tears. "You gave your life for me, but your contract isn't up. You're what they call a shade. A ghost stuck on the earthly plane."

A tilt of his head as he studied my floating spirit. "Are you here to bring me back?"

"I wish I could. I do have to return." Then, to whoever might be listening at SMG, "I will not leave them. Justice must be served."

"Yes," Death agreed. He was in my head, all around me. "It's not your time."

"Nor is it his." I sounded calm, reasonable. I meant both Killion and Pennyworth.

As if I had summoned him, I heard the master vampire say, "Wake."

I came back from the Land of the Dead with a rush. No longer in the penthouse, I blinked up at the Gothic chandelier overhead in the rafters of a familiar looking church. St. Anne's——a place out of space and time. It had once been real but magic had taken over and it had eventually been commandeered by Killion. It was part safe haven, part interrogation site. Katarina lived and worked here. It was where she regularly beat the reaper out of me during our training sessions.

I'd never been happier to see it.

"Welcome back," Aurora said. Her face was pale but her eyes lit up when I glanced her way. She flashed a relieved smile.

Killion helped me to sit, the action slow due to my

achy body and foggy brain. Katarina handed me a paper cup of something. The liquid glowed with magic.

"How do you feel?" Killion asked.

They all looked drained, but him especially. His face was lined, his energy depleted. Part, I knew, was because of my death. Not only was our emotional bond eternal, we were literally tied together physically. When I finally and truly died, he would, too.

I drank down the magical water in two unladylike gulps, sighing at its coolness even as I screwed up my nose from the taste. Wiping off my wet chin from the overflow, I blinked away the last of the fogginess. "I've been better. You?"

"Same." He hugged me to him in an almost vicious grasp, then set me back. "You have to stop doing that."

"What, dying?" I offered a smile. It was weak, and we both knew it. Handing the empty cup to Aurora, I asked, "What was that?"

She accepted it and surveyed me with a physician's eye. "It will help you get your strength back. The stake was soaked in Belladonna and Wolfsbane, along with whatever venom Sable possesses. You and the vampire are lucky to be alive."

Killion couldn't stop touching me. He took my hand and I threaded my fingers through his. "Death had to resurrect you. We weren't sure you could do it yourself."

Death. Where was he? Where was my dog? "Ghost? Is she here?"

At the sound of my voice, she came running. I heard her bark and pushed off the communion table that had acted like a bed. Stooping, I opened my arms and hugged her to me, fighting the dizziness that caused me to sway. Killion steadied me as she licked my face. It was so *normal*, I laughed.

It was good to be alive. It felt wrong to have left Pennyworth dead. "Cron and Mags?"

Killion shook his head. "The stakes were poisoned."

"We didn't reach them in time," Katarina said, an edge to her voice. "Not sure we could have saved them even if we had."

"It's nasty stuff." I leaned against the table, heart aching, and placed the dog next to me. "What about Lasarus and Sable's friend? The one Pepper killed?"

"Taken care of," Killion assured me. "The clinic has been cleaned and returned to normal."

"They're after you," I told him. "I'm so sorry about Pennyworth."

Katarina took the cup from Aurora and crushed it with one hand. "They will die, slowly and miserably."

I might not be one for torture, but at that moment, I was willing to put my feelings aside and cheer her on. "Where's my scythe?"

Killion glanced at Katarina. "We will deal with the strigoi. You stay here and recover."

"I'm recovered. And they're going to wish I wasn't. Where's the blade?"

"About that." Death appeared out of thin air, startling all of us. I swear, he loves to do that. "We have a problem."

I had more than I could count. "I didn't mean to trash Mei's office. It wasn't me, anyway. It was Stormfinger, and if you'd told me who I was dealing with—"

"Stormfinger?" Aurora and Killion chorused in unison.

"He's the ghost haunting SMG." I glanced at my boss. "Just a wild guess, but I'd say he's pissed about that little Act of God lightning bolt that ended him."

"We'll discuss your penchant for destruction and chaos later. Our foremost issue at the moment is the fact you let an unauthorized entity steal your scythe."

I gaped. "What?"

Katarina cleared her throat, looking a tad sheepish even through her anger. "Sable still has it."

Death crooked a finger at me before striding for the exit, his long legs eating up the aisle. "You and I are going to retrieve it."

"She's not ready for a fight," Killion said, staying my hand as I went to pick up Ghost.

"Come, Grim," Death called. "Bring your lapdog with you."

He wasn't talking about the psychopomp and we all knew it. Killion bared his teeth at Death's back.

I placed a hand on his chest, sending a trickle of my magic into his heart, right at the location where mine still throbbed from the stabbing. "We'll all go."

He leaned his forehead against mine. "This is a bad idea. I can handle them on my own."

"I know." I gave him a fierce nod of agreement. "But I need to do this. For Pennyworth." His name made my heart ache all over again.

"For Pennyworth," he echoed.

Katarina and Aurora joined us as Killion and I followed Death. "For Pennyworth," they chorused.

Just before we hit the exit, a ghost appeared right in front of me. I jumped and gave a shriek.

"May I come?" the butler asked, looking positively excited in his floating spirit form. "I do love a good fight."

Aurora laughed and Katarina swore under her breath, both of them able to see him. "Tell me you're not going to haunt my church now," the enforcer admonished good-naturedly.

The ghost vampire grinned and swooped up into the high ceiling, then back down, whizzing around us. "It's actually kind of fun to be dead. Like, *really* dead. Poor Omwee. Has anyone told him?"

"I did," Katarina said. "Harlow is with him now. When he's ready, we'll plan a memorial."

Harlow was Killion's second in command and Mason's mother. I was relieved that Pennyworth's grieving partner had her by his side.

The butler waved a ghostly hand. "I don't need one."

"Yes, you do," I insisted. "The food will suck, though."

He tried to pinch my cheek and his cold hand went right through me. He winked instead.

Killion gave a long-suffering sigh. "Come on, then, Pennyworth. It's your retribution as much as ours."

We found Andy outside keeping a good distance between him and Death. My boss tapped an impatient foot. "You're not going," he said to the others. "This is Chloe's responsibility."

"Sure we are." Andy moved to Aurora's side and placed a supportive hand on her lower back. "Chloe comes with a lot of baggage. You know that."

I grinned at the frustration on Death's face. "What he means is, I have great friends."

"And deadly enemies," my boss reminded me.

"Those, too," I admitted. "And it's time we taught them a lesson."

FIFTEEN

The setting sun threw weak streams of yellow and peach over us as we gathered in the front of the church to form a plan. Katarina's pets—two big dogs I'd accidentally resurrected a few months ago—ran from their graveyard playground and greeted us with wet muzzles and panting. Ghost tolerated them, but pawed me to lift her out of the fray.

I did so, planting a kiss on the top of her head while petting the two big dogs, one Lab and one Golden Retriever, who circled my feet and checked my hands for treats. "Sorry, I'm fresh out," I told them.

Killion stayed close by my side as he addressed Death. "Where exactly are we going? We can take my limo."

"Tap into your magic," my boss instructed me. "You have a direct connection to your scythe. Where is it?"

Katarina's pets decided I wasn't worth much if I didn't provide food and returned to the graveyard. Setting Ghost down and closing my eyes, I dipped into the power thrumming through my system. After dying, it should have been weak, but slipping into the void seemed to have recharged parts of me.

My power instantly responded.

Sending out tendrils of magic in all directions, I searched for the blade. A cacophony of information came back, but none from my weapon. All of the sensations, sounds, and visions were linked to living people as well as the dead. "I can't find it."

Killion's magic slipped into me, winding around mine. "Don't try to find the steel. Search for your essence within it."

Whatever *that* meant. I tried again. *Where are you?* I knew the others were watching, waiting for me to declare its location along with the strigoi, but I sensed neither. I opened my eyes and shrugged. "I've got nothing. Usually, I can hear it in my head."

Aurora gave me a funny look. "You never told me that. Hear it how?"

"It sort of talks."

"Cool." Andy grinned. "What does it say?"

"I know this may be a shocker, but the only thing it ever says is *kill*." They looked vaguely amused. I glanced at the master vampire. "Can you tune in to it through me?"

He shook his head. "Afraid not. If you can't find it, I cannot either."

A muscle twitched in Death's jaw. "You have the ability, Chloe. Call to it."

"Surely you do, too," I countered. "Why don't you?"

His whole jaw clinched. "It is *your* weapon."

From his reaction and the way he gritted his teeth, I realized he couldn't sense it. This seemed to annoy him as much as my impertinence.

He was death incarnate, yet did not carry weapons of any kind. He relied on reapers to harvest souls, even though he had power over life and death. Aurora had told me the Fae did not like iron; was it possible Death did not care for steel?

All eyes jumped between us. Deciding this was a fight I wouldn't win, I closed mine once more, tunneling into myself and searching for the link. If it called to me, talked to me, I could do the same to it, right? *Where are you? I need you.*

My magic swept out in a circle, flowing over the ground, through trees, around buildings, all the way to the edge of town. The dead, both in their graves and those haunting the earth, responded, their souls coming to attention as my necromantic magic caressed them.

"Chloe...?" Aurora's voice was tense. She could feel them, too. "Be careful."

Rest, I said to the sentient souls. I certainly didn't want an army of zombies rising all around us. *Sleep, my children.*

My children? *Where had that come from?* Killion's hand squeezed mine. Oh right. Grim Zero. My alter ego loved the dead and felt as though she was their mother.

A chill swept over my skin and raced down my spine. I felt her move, eyes opening. Awareness honing in on me, her magic waking up.

Now it was Killion who gave me a warning. "While

she may be able to detect the blade, bringing her through would be a mistake."

"You think? It's not like I'm trying to rouse her." Drawing in a deep, studying breath, I refocused on the scythe, seeing it in my mind's eye. I lowered the intensity of my power, combing through my magic and pulling several strands back. Soothing Grim Zero. *Sorry to disturb you. We're all good here. Just a hiccup.*

She quieted, but didn't return to her normal slumbering state. She seemed to study me. Waiting. Watching. *What are you up to?*

I froze at her voice echoing in my ears. Purring almost.

Killion stilled as well. Across the way, I felt Death do the same.

Nothing, I insisted. *My friend died. I'm upset. My magic is wonky, and I accidentally agitated you. Sorry.*

Wonky? Her smooth, unruffled voice flowed over my brain and settled in my chest. *Explain.*

"What's happening?" Aurora whispered. "Is Chloe okay?"

"I'm fine," I said aloud. "Just chatting with Grim Zero."

I sensed the witch cringe. Even with my eyes shut, I knew Andy took a step back. Katarina's magic rose in alarm. I didn't blame them for their fear.

In my mind, I addressed her again. *Wonky is a term we use to mean uncontrolled. When I get emotional, that's what happens—I lose control of my magic. I'm still learning.*

Grim Zero: *Until you let it out to play and understand*

what you can do with it, it will continue to become 'wonky.' The word sounded odd coming from her.

She was probably right, but taking the restraints off my magic was, in essence, taking them off her. We all knew what she wanted to do with the world, to it, and I wasn't going to let that happen. *Time for me to get back to work. You must return to sleep.*

As Aurora and Killion had insisted, I had befriended her as much as I possibly could. I avoided confronting her, but I'd discovered that unless I asserted my dominance, she would push me around. By nature, I wasn't aggressive or bossy. With her, I had to be.

For a moment, she said nothing. I sensed her stretching, cat-like. Once more, she purred, *I can help you find Kill.*

It was my turn to pause. *You named the blade?*

She hummed, pleased. *It is a sentient being. You name things that aren't.*

Like the espresso machine. My car. The items were left unsaid, yet I knew that was her point.

Well, wasn't this an *aha* moment. The scythe had a name, had been trying to tell me that all along. Maybe that was also why Corvus constantly shouted, "Kill."

Me: *Your help is appreciated. I'll take things from here.*

Immediately, I shut down the link. I didn't want to slam it into place but sometimes had to. Doing so was like shoving a pitchfork into my brain. I reeled a bit from the pain and grabbed my skull.

Killion held me. One hand on my elbow, the other on

my lower back, he sent a wave of magic into my body, calming it as well as my nerves.

Death scoffed. "You never realized the scythe had a name as well as a purpose?"

Leaning on the master vampire felt good, but I reluctantly pushed away. "You never bothered to tell me. I think you prefer it that way. You want to keep me off balance, punish me with these petty little details. Pop in when you're least expected." *Or wanted.* "Does it make you feel superior?"

Andy had indeed taken a step back. He took another, dragging Aurora with him. Probably a good move, since Death stalked with immortal but lethal grace toward me and glared into my eyes. *"Find the blade."*

I started to argue, but Killion sent another ripple of magic out. This one protective, a shield. The three of us—four, if you included Grim Zero—were locked in this never-ending dance. None of us could ever truly have the ultimate power over the others, yet the struggle would always be there.

My goals were not the same as Death's, and though he and I were intricately linked forever, we would also forever be at odds with each other.

I didn't back down from his glower. "Give me a minute, will you? I've never had to do this before."

He marched away and I breathed easier. Killion, always the steadying force—and often the less volatile of us, kept his calm and protective demeanor. He believed I could locate the scythe, but rather than demand my obedience, he offered patience and reassurance.

I nodded at him and closed my eyes yet again. It

helped me focus. I nudged my magic gently and reached out with it, searching for the thread that bound me to the blade.

I felt a tickle in my chest. *Kill?*

It didn't respond, but Grim Zero did, blasting through the door I had shut on her. Wave after wave of her necromantic power rolled through me, out of me. Gritting my teeth, I resisted, trying to latch onto it and stuff it into the hole where I kept her.

She laughed somewhere in the back of my brain and I gripped Killion hard, staggering from her power. On a knife's edge, I danced with her and her magic. She teased me. "Stop it," I ground out.

Kill, she called and something flickered on the fringe of my vision. Cold steel, silvery and *awake*.

Instinctively, I turned my head, even though my eyes were closed. The blade of silver blinked out. I swore under my breath.

"What's happening?" Aurora asked.

Swiveling my head to the front, I started to answer, but stopped when that flicker appeared off to my right again. I couldn't look directly at it, but it flared on the margin of my peripheral vision.

Do you see? Grim Zero spoke. Not to me—to Death. *Do you know?*

"Yes," I heard him say.

Without warning, she shut down our link, the sensation similar to her punching me right in the gut. I sucked air and doubled over, hearing the faint echo of her laugh. Was this what she felt when I did the same to her?

That thought was put on hold when, in the next

moment, I became nothing more than dust in the air, streaming through space.

When my particles reformed into a physical body, I staggered and nearly vomited. Around me, the others were doing the same.

Everyone, that is, except for the being who had brought us here and my mate. Death surveyed the landscape, unbothered.

Killion reached for me since we had become disconnected while being transported. Andy and Aurora leaned on each other as well. Katarina cursed, her voice vibrating around us. Little Ghost wagged her tail and began sniffing the barren ground.

It was brighter here, the sun cutting sharply as it made its descent in the distance. I blinked, holding my belly. Killion helped me straighten and replaced my hand with his, soothing the throbbing there.

A hawk cried in the distance and Ghost lifted her head and barked. We all took in the view, high on a giant hill above a forest. While the woods displayed plenty of life, the ground on which we stood was dry and brown, a few single trees skeletal and rotted.

"What is this place?" I asked.

Pennyworth appeared next to me. "DuMort Hill."

"Hey," I said. "Glad you could make it." As I slowly turned in a circle, I could see for miles. A clear demarcation of dead grass and trees spread in all directions, clearly separating our spot from the natural, and very alive, area beyond it.

Louisiana didn't have many mountains, and this one probably wasn't far enough above sea level to qualify, but the air here was thinner and I found it taxing to breathe deeply.

"I've heard of this place," Aurora said. "The hill of death."

I watched my boss for any sign of acknowledgement. He continued to scan the landscape, clearly aggravated. There was no sign of the strigoi.

I was both disappointed and relieved. "You have a hill named after you?" I tried to sound teasing but failed. "How...depressing."

Four giant stones anchored the circle, crosses carved into them. A slight buzzing sensation tickled my feet through my boots and pricked my skin like sleet. Killion sensed it, too, shooting me a concerned and wary glance.

"Native tribes used this site for ceremonies," Pennyworth said, floating over a giant marker. "They even performed sacrifices and buried the dead right here."

"Explorers brought disease." Aurora rubbed her arms as if chilled. "And subjugation. The Spanish, then the French, invaded. There was a notable skirmish fought here."

Pennyworth moved to the stone farthest from us. Ghost trailed after him, nose on the ground. "The only native left after that battle was a shaman. He cursed the French Army and the land, claiming no crops would ever grow. That the conquerors who had slain his people would never bare children. That everything they touched would turn to dust."

"How do you know that?" Andy asked.

Pennyworth gave him an odd look. "I read. Don't you?"

Aurora jabbed the shifter in the side. "History is important. This place *is* cursed. When a group of monks erected a monastery here in the early 1900s,"—she pointed at the foundation stones—"they thought they could prove God's power would overcome the decades of death that had existed. They prayed and worked the land, blessing it on the first of each month, but it never yielded anything. One by one, they died from mysterious ailments or simply disappeared. The Church claimed they moved on, but there was gossip that said differently."

"Great." I began dragging Killion away. "I suggest we get out of this circle. Come, Ghost."

"Nothing will harm you." It was the first words Death had spoken since transporting us. "Where is the blade?"

A dog with a bone. Killion and I continued to backtrack away from the center of the hill. Ghost worked her way toward us in no hurry. Katarina moved to the west, her own nose seeming to test the air, her vampire vision inspecting every inch of ground. If the strigoi were near, she'd detect them.

I felt, rather than saw, the sun begin to dip below the horizon.

The scythe was nowhere visible, and there were far too many bones and bodies under my feet for me to feel comfortable. Regardless that my alter ego wanted to raise them all, it was simply creepy. "Maybe Grim Zero was wrong," I said. "Maybe she's playing a game with us."

Wouldn't be the first time.

Death shook his head. "It's here. We must find it."

Killion gazed into the distance. "We aren't far from the arboretum where we found the bodies."

"The last owners of this acreage were farmers," Death said. "Obviously, that was a poor choice of career for this place. When crop after crop failed, they set up a greenhouse half a mile south. Eventually, the next owners turned it into an arboretum for the public, until the husband passed. It was too much for his wife to keep up."

Beneath my feet, the dead began to stir. They sensed my presence, and perhaps Aurora's necromancy, as well. The lifeless grass around me shivered; the faintest touch of green slipped into the brown, as if by the stroke of a paintbrush.

I felt the souls of those under us become agitated. "I don't mean to break up the party, but I think it's time we get off this hill. For real. Things beneath me are waking up."

"We have to find your weapon," Death insisted, but it was without annoyance this time. He studied the ground, as if thinking something over, and frowned.

I shivered at the idea that crossed my mind at his studiousness. "No way. You think they buried it? Here?"

"It is Death's Hill," Andy said.

I pivoted, releasing my grip on Killion. "Can't be. We'd be able to see if they had disturbed the area."

Death continued to inspect the earth, and now the others did as well. While shadows crept around the tree line of the distant forest, there was little here to cause any. The air buzzed with dark energy.

There was no overturned soil, no sign of any kind of burial. Ghost showed no intent of tracking the blade.

"Spread out," Killion commanded. "Check every inch of the space." To me, he said, "If you can't control your necromancy, it would be best for you to wait in the woods."

I bit my bottom lip, debating. I *could* control it, and as Death had reminded me, it was *my* blade. I had to help. "Let me try something," I said to the group.

All eyes met mine, each pausing, wary.

Okay, Kill, I said mentally, sending out my own flicker of magic like a beacon. *I'm here. Show me where you are.*

Beneath my feet, the ground shook.

SIXTEEN

Katarina yelped, Andy shifted into wolf form, and Pennyworth said, "Uh oh."

Ghost barked, the sound too loud in my ears, as she seemed to remind me we'd *been here, done this*, only hours before in Mei's office.

The sun had relinquished the day and night rolled over us. Controlling my breathing and my magic, I hummed. Nothing fancy, just a pop tune that had been stuck in my brain since my coffee shop shift. Mason had played it twice while I'd been there.

While I'd ignored it then, now it soothed me. Killion had told me once during a particularly intense session with Katarina that music could help me shut off the overly logical part of my brain and allow my instincts to take over.

The bodies below continued to shift. Ignoring my inner cringe at the sound of my voice, I hummed louder. *Now is not the time to rise. Listen to the soft sound of my humming and be at peace.*

The shaking eased. Just a bit, but it motivated me. I kept it up, and at the same time, I let go of a trickle of magic. Like Killion had suggested, the blade held my essence. I called to it. "Here kitty, kitty, kitty."

Katarina had circled around to us, ready to defend her master. "Kitty?"

"*Here Kill* doesn't have the same nice ring." I turned to the left, attention on the ground. "I've come to rescue you. Where are you?"

Often during fights with noncompliant souls, I held out my hand and the blade was drawn to it like a magnet to steel. This time, only cool air brushed over my palm.

"I don't think it likes being called *kitty*," Aurora said. Andy snorted.

I had a different worry. "What if it's changed allegiance?" I quirked a brow at Death. "Is that possible? I mean, it once belonged to Avi. Now me. What if it decided it likes Sable better?"

He crossed his arms. "You're Grim Zero. Every scythe will respond to you. Kill's allegiance didn't change; it simply recognized you as its rightful owner."

Ghost's head came up and her lips quivered in a silent growl. Alerted, I glanced in the direction she stared. My own hackles rose.

The others followed suit. In the distance along the tree line stood a shadowed figure. Although I couldn't see her features, I immediately knew who it was. "Sable."

Moonlight glinted off steel, then the sound of her laughter echoed to us. She darted into the trees.

I was running before I took my next breath. Killion was at my side. Katarina darted past us, a blur. Ghost, equally as fast, caught up to her. In the background, I heard Death snarl, "Get back here."

I might have made a rather rude gesture over my shoulder at him. Sometimes my fingers did things all on their own. *Oops.*

The ground under me barely registered, Killion's shared speed making me fly across the field and into the trees. Katarina disappeared far ahead of us and I realized that even though I was moving faster than I ever had, Killion had slowed his natural speed in order to stay by my side. What freedom it was, though!

I nearly laughed as I easily dodged enormous tree trunks and fallen branches. Having been a klutz for so long, and always sucking at gym, I sort of wished all my former classmates, especially those who'd made fun of me, could see me now.

This could be a trap. Killion's voice in my head did not carry any suggestion we should stop; only be prepared.

With barely a thought, I knew he was right. I sensed it. *This* is *a trap. What should we do?*

He wasn't simply a master vampire because of his bloodline—he was logical, strategic, cool-headed. He'd lived centuries, fought in battles, survived the overthrow of kingdoms. He'd led others in ancient and modern times, and he knew Lasarus. *Katarina is scouting. We wait for her report.*

He slowed. I did, too. Motioning me to follow, he advanced on silent feet, leading me off the path that Sable had taken, even as he sniffed the air like a blood-hound and tracked her scent.

We moved within range of the deserted arboretum. I didn't have a telepathic link with Katarina, but knew Killion was getting the lay of the land from her. I started to send a wave of magic out to see if I could tell how many entities were inside, if any, but he stopped me. *I do not want them to sense your presence.*

Them. More than one. *How many?*

He held up a hand, asking me to wait. His brows furrowed.

And that's when I felt the earthy but not-of-this-world magic of the Fae. At the same time, the vampires must have picked up on the scent.

There had been no pulse of magic, like Harmony had used in the bar, but the swoon-y looks they suddenly wore were identical to those the previous night. "Are the Fae *and* the strigoi here?" I whispered.

Killion shook his head. "It seems no one is at this moment, but both have been. Recently."

He led me around to the double-doored entryway. A pane of the immense glass on the left had been busted out long ago. The metal squawked as he tugged open a panel. Katarina grabbed the other and it, too, protested when she yanked on it.

A wave of dry rot and dead things filled my nostrils. I held my breath until I adjusted my vision to peer into the gloom of the abandoned and falling down building. It had been quite a show piece in its heyday, yet now was long forgotten.

Except for the vampires—and Fae—using it as a repository for those they'd killed.

While I had a general sense of the blueprint from my

previous visit here with Killion, I longed for a flashlight. The creeping vegetation from the surrounding forest blocked the remnants of the moon, and my vision wasn't as accurate as the two vampires and Ghost.

Killion and Katarina sniffed the air. I mimicked them, but the strigoi's stench was overwhelmed by the structure's decay. I still couldn't detect that of the Fae. Had the two groups been working together?

Killion led me through the interior labyrinth of long dead trees, bushes, and trailing plants that had filled the interior. A few statues lingered, some broken by vandals, others moss covered and stained from rain. The whole place had a sad, forlorn air to it.

Residual magic became visible to me, as did a few specters. The latter hid, sensing who I was, and I did my best to ignore them. I had more important things to take care of.

I drew out my phone and turned on the flashlight. Killion said nothing, continuing to use his own version of night vision rather than my thin beam as he lead us deeper into the building.

Focusing, I sent out a whisper of magic to check for the scythe. It flowed through the area like a soft stream, but all I sensed were the long-dead plants stirring. I withdrew it and stumbled on.

Glass crunched behind me and I jerked so hard, I nearly dropped the cell. Andy, in wolf form, tongue out as if he'd ran all the way here, flinched when the light cut across his eyes.

"Sorry," I said, lowering it. "As you can probably sniff out, both the strigoi and the Fae have been here. Any chance you can put your nose to use and see if you can figure out if they hid my blade before they left?"

He pawed the ground once—our signal for *yes*.

Neither Aurora, nor Death, joined us. I continued to follow Killion, weaving around one of the tiled fountains with a naked cupid-like statue in the center. Pretty sure I didn't want to know where the stream of water for that poured from when it was in working condition. A bar of light from my phone swept his face, his grin near lifelike. With the stains on his chubby cheeks and moss growing on his you-know-what, it totally freaked me out.

I ran into Killion's back when he pulled up. He glanced at me and frowned. "What is it?"

"Nothing. Just a creepy statue." I shivered. "If Sable hid Kill in here, shouldn't I sense him?"

"At the moment, I am more interested in discovering what Lasarus and the Fae have been doing together."

"Hunting?" I asked.

"Hmm," was his only reply.

Were we about to find more bodies?

A sticky sweet sensation hit my spine, the sound of footsteps behind me sending me spinning around, raising my phone as much for the light as a weapon.

"Fair evening," a male voice said, the male squinted at the illumination. His sensuous Fae magic slid and danced up my back, vertebrae by vertebrae. "I mean no harm."

That remained to be seen. "Prince Oz?" I lowered the device. "What are you doing here?"

Killion was instantly beside me. "Where are the others?"

"Wish I knew." He looked dour in the glow. "I was told to meet the vampires here."

"You're working together," Killion accused. "Why?"

The prince looked taken aback. "I would not lower myself to give them the time of day, much less work with them."

Katarina emerged from the gloom, a shadow herself. The white of her fangs shone when she spat, "Liar."

He went very still—one apex predator sizing up another. "They've taken my cousin. That is why I am here."

"The princess?" Ghost, in her psychopomp form, strutted up to me. "What for?"

"I thought for ransom, or perhaps to create a bargain with my family. The message came to meet them here, yet"—he held out his arms at the decaying place—"I only find you."

That sounded an awful lot like an accusation. "We had nothing to do with—"

"Ambush," Killion yelled, at the same moment I felt an odd pressure in my head. "Get out!"

He had just enough time to push me toward the exit before the place exploded.

SEVENTEEN

The eruption lifted me off my feet and shot me through the air. Time slowed.

Windows that had still been intact shattered into hundreds of glass daggers. They flew at me, cutting my exposed skin.

Killion morphed in mid-reach for me, his body becoming all fangs and claws and blood red eyes. Not completely vampire, nor dragon, but something in-between. His inner monster took over to protect him, and in essence, me.

I catapulted through the darkness, the fiery ball of the detonation lighting the night, then winking out, leaving the stars overhead reflecting on the shattered jagged panes. My ears throbbed and blood seeped from them, ringing with a high-pitched squeal.

Bones crunched when my back slammed into a giant oak several yards from the cupid, the pain so all-consuming I screamed. The sound seemed distant, muffled to my damaged hearing.

After impact, I dropped to the ground and Killion landed on top of me. The weight and sheer force of his beast knocked the air from my battered lungs, making me shriek again. Dozens of glass knives as big as my hands drove into us. He covered me, the razor sharp weapons embedding themselves deep in his back.

Unable to breathe, to speak, all I could do was lie there. My body and brain were in shock. The echo of the explosion reverberated in my ears and magic like a living thing. I felt frozen, unable to do more than blink.

Even that hurt.

The half-beast did not cry out from the glass in his spine, but his breathing was harsh, ragged. He, too, seemed frozen, unable to move, his gaze pinned on the ground next to my head.

Killion, I whispered mentally, seeking him with my magic. It seemed fragmented and almost...burnt. My mouth tasted of ashes and loss.

His silent agony mingled with mine. I sensed the edginess of his inner beast trying to hold onto the last shreds of his humanity. I prayed he could, because if not, I would become food for his dragon.

Fear creeped along my broken body—not of him, but of what had happened. Katarina. Andy. Ghost. *Are they alive?*

The deafening silence sent fear sliding through me.

Killion. I pushed a stronger force into it this time. My magic swirled, the fragments melding. My natural healing sputtered, went out, flickered to life again.

Concentrating, I flooded him with all I had. Black spots danced on the edges of my vision and more fiery agony lanced through me, causing me to nearly lose consciousness.

With no warning, Grim Zero burst through the wall I'd secured between us, forcing me to inhale. Raw fire hit my shattered ribs and I regretted sucking in another sharp breath as her magic began to knit bones back together.

The pain! Searing, horrible torment. With oxygen filling my lungs, I issued a feeble sob. The monster's attention snapped to me. *Live,* he growled inside my head. A command.

His blood soaked my clothes, mixing with my own. I stared into his eyes and his breathing became harsher, more erratic. I still couldn't find his magic, yet sensed it was *right there*.

Live, I fired back. I infused the order with Grim Zero's power this time, feeling momentary satisfaction as it rushed through each of us.

The intensity of it was a combination of torture and relief. A key fitting into a lock. As it took hold, the red glow of Killion's irises didn't diminish, but I glimpsed specs of violet in them.

Inside me, Grim Zero shoved me into a corner with the ease of batting away a fly. "It is not your time, vampire master," she said through my lips.

My ears stopped ringing and I lifted a previously broken hand to place it on his scaled chest. The moment it came into contact with him, a bluish glow emanated from them. The sensation was icy cold and fiery hot at the same time. More flecks appeared in his eyes.

The embedded glass in his shoulders and back began

to move, muscles and tendons healing and forcing out the pieces. Each was ejected with such force, it sailed through the air. Grim Zero's magic knocked them aside as easily as she had me. My hand—controlled by her—waved over Killion's bleeding backside and the wounds healed instantly.

Her power both terrified and excited me, yet in that moment, what I felt most was gratitude. She had saved us.

The crunch of glass under feet drew my attention. "What the bloody hell?"

Death stood over us and her attention switched to him. He watched with no small amount of wonder as she used me as a means to heal Killion. A place inside my chest warmed as she stared at Death and I felt an unwelcome sense of bonding blossoming there.

"Andy!" Aurora screamed, racing up to us. When she saw the beast on top of me, she covered her mouth with a hand and stepped back. She glanced around. "Where is he? Where is Andy?"

Grim Zero cared little for the shifter or my psychopomp. All she wanted in that moment was to greet her soulmate. "Death," she crooned, and I watched as he realized it was her in charge of my body.

Aurora swore as she, too, discerned who was speaking. Deciding to stay out of it, and concerned for her lover, she charged into the debris to find the wolf.

"It's been a while," Death said. Neutral, emotionless. He studied me, then spoke to the monster. "Killion, can you stand?"

Slowly, Killion tamed his dragon, becoming more

vampire again. He shifted onto his elbows. The weight lifted off me, and inch by inch, he crawled away, remaining scales flashing off and on with that blue glow. He crawled into the trees and I called to him, but nothing came out, neither verbally nor telepathically. Grim Zero had silenced me.

My broken body continued to repair itself and she forced me to sit up, a smile curving my lips. In the background, I heard Aurora shouting and sobbing—Andy was dead.

Tears welled in my eyes for him, for Ghost. I assumed she hadn't survived either. What of Katarina? Of Oz? Had they, too, been killed?

As quickly as the tears came, they dried. My alter ego didn't tolerate displays of weakness or emotions, even though hers ran so very, very deep.

"Thank you for saving Chloe and Killion," Death said. He made no move to help her—me—up. "I'll handle it from here."

The warmth in my chest went cold. She wasn't one to be dismissed. I sensed a building of her magic, heady and beyond the power she'd already displayed. It was as if she were reaching into a bottomless well, tugging it up to unleash. "We are partners."

The words carried such weight it dragged down my bones. To her, he was much more than a *partner*. They were bonded.

"We are." Death nodded. "At the moment, however, I need Chloe. You and I will talk soon. I know you have much to say, and I..." He loosed a breath. "I will listen."

Grim Zero chuckled low and vicious. She brought me

to my feet. "When have you ever listened to me? When have you ever treated me as your equal?"

He inclined his head, offering sufficient pause to digest her words. "You've always held more power. I'm sorry I wasn't there when you needed me. I am to blame for what happened and I will always carry that burden. You and I must find a way to exist with each other in a new world, and we must not upset the balance of it as we do so."

The ice inside my chest thawed slightly. She hesitated in her tunneling into her ocean of magic. Her grief softened. Not completely, but I realized she needed hope, and he'd just offered it to her.

Through my eyes, she glanced around at the destruction. Under my feet, I felt more of the dead stir, but she instantly silenced them. So easy for her. "One chance," she told him, hating herself for believing his words. Believing he still cared. "You get only one. Make it count. Find us a way in which to coexist again."

With that she was gone, resurrecting the barrier all on her own. It left me staggering.

Strong hands gripped me from behind to stop my fall. I turned to find Killion there. The beast was one hundred percent gone.

My nerves buzzed as if I'd downed three espressos and I wrapped my arms around his neck. "Are you okay?" My voice was hoarse, barely above a whisper, but it was mine, not hers. Small miracles.

"I will be." He stroked the back of my head and tiny glass shards tinkled to the ground. "Is she...?"

I nodded, holding him a moment longer before

forcing myself to release him and face Death. Everything in me ached, burned, each movement a tiny fire.

"Nice speech," I said to Death. It was all I could get out.

Then I went to comfort my friend, still sobbing over Andy.

EIGHTEEN

There wasn't much left of the wolf, Aurora bent over his bleeding form. Ghost was nowhere to be seen and I called her name over and over as I ambled around on weak legs, bracing myself for the discovery of her pinned under a piece of statue or skewered by glass.

Killion hunted for Katarina, no doubt prepping himself for a similar discovery. Death, grinding his teeth audibly, stomped past me, seemingly unable to take in the extent of what had happened, or perhaps doing his best to contain his anger at the strigoi.

I suspected he was also chewing over when and how he was going to have that promised conversation with Grim Zero. While he certainly couldn't be looking forward to it, I was definitely dreading it.

Soft words flowed from Aurora's mouth. Her necromancy tickled my nose and raised the tiny hairs on the back of my neck as she murmured a spell.

"Stop," Death ordered. "Do not raise him. Just

because you have the ability doesn't mean you should use it. That is not your domain."

She ignored him and goosebumps raced over my skin with the desire to join her. There was a millennium of the dead there in the space and they called to me.

Beings that had dissolved into dust eons ago began to reform.

I fell to my knees beside her, gritting my teeth against the lure of using my own necro powers. I didn't dare touch her, but needed to break her focus. Her magic was tangled with her emotions, and she wasn't keeping it directed only at the dead wolf. "This isn't the answer," I said, gritting my teeth against it. The lure was so inviting. "You are going to raise more than Andy."

Her head lifted and I gasped at the ice blue eyes of her panther staring back at me. "Leave me be. I will not lose him."

Behind the wall inside me, Grim Zero chuckled. *If you were a true friend, you would help her.*

Clenching and unclenching my hands, I walked a fine line between consoling her and giving into her wishes. "I understand," I said, my skin itching as her magic slid over it, "but this isn't the way."

The panther snarled. "You would do the same for *him*."

Killion. I would, too. I was pretty sure I just had—with a little help from my true self.

She held her hands out over Andy's ravaged body and I grabbed them, risking what she might do to me. My fingers instantly froze, but I held on as she tried to jerk away.

"Let go," she demanded.

This could end our friendship. She would hate me forever. Probably curse me. I tightened my grip, grinding my teeth against the icy heat racing like wildfire up my arms and into my chest and neck. The dead beneath me howled in my mind, ready to rise and defend me. "You are raising more than Andy. I can't let you do that."

Her eyes blazed with anger, hurt, betrayal. Yep, I was cursed for sure. "*Let. Go.*"

"No." I accepted her necromancy, as well as her anger and pain. In return, I flooded her with my life-giving energy. Not to raise the dead, only to soothe the living.

Grim Zero approved, but only because she slipped hers into the stream of it, sending it toward Andy and the spirits waking up.

I fought her, reeling back. Slapping her magic away like she had me earlier, I wound mine around my friend's heart and she loosed a sob. Her fight was fierce but brief, before she finally crumpled and fell into my arms.

I held her and rocked her as she cried. Over her shoulder, Death offered a nod of encouragement. Grief racked her body, yet I hated myself for betraying her.

Clouds skirted across the stars and we were drenched in darkness. I reached out mentally to Killion. *Any luck?*

No.

A single word, yet the emotions it contained held a universe. Katarina was part of his family. A family he would do anything for, protect at all costs. Her death, on top of Pennyworth's, was shredding his heart.

And it was my fault.

My own felt as if it could not contain the sorrow of all we had lost this night. The heavy weight of it crept into my veins, pumped through my chest, squeezed my lungs.

Gone. They were all gone—Pennyworth, Andy, Ghost, Katarina. Even Kill and Ozmeus. I closed my eyes against the enormity of it, but it leaked out as tears, streaming down my face.

Hot, stinky breath hit me and I opened my eyes to see those of my psychopomp's staring me down. Drool dripped from her open mouth and she cocked her head sideways.

"Ghost?" I sat back in surprise, dislodging Aurora.

Beside the dog stood Andy in human form. Not a specter—he was alive. His hand was on her collar, they both looked like cats who'd eaten more than one canary.

"I'm back," Andy said with a smug air.

Aurora hiccupped, jumping to her feet. She pivoted and shrieked all in one breath and then pointed a shaky finger at him. "How... What...?"

He grinned wickedly. "Soul Management Group sent me back." His shoulders rose and fell in a casual shrug. "That Mei Han gal is a hundred levels of afterlife scary. Said I owed her,"—he glanced my way—"and you, Chloe. She ordered me to return and use my tracking skills, sort of like a contractor, I guess, to complete three tasks for her."

Aurora threw her arms around him, making him laugh as he caught her in a hug. The sight made me smile.

Mimicking her, I wrapped mine around Ghost and squeezed her tight. "Holy reapers, dog. I thought you were dead."

Death marched over. "She's a psychopomp. Nearly impossible to kill."

Narrowing my eyes at him, I released her, but kept a hand on her shoulder. "You never told me that."

"Section 6 1 0 of the manual. I thought you said you read it."

"I have. Several times. I've never seen anything stating psychopomps are immortal." I suspected by the way he wouldn't meet my eyes that he was making it up. There were lots of codes and rules I'd glossed over due to their yawn-worthy nature, but any having to do with my dog had been read thoroughly.

Death pinned Andy with a serious stare. "What tasks?"

"Um." The shifter broke free from Aurora's embrace but accepted the kiss she laid on his cheek. "I'm the fixer, remember? One is to help Chloe retrieve her scythe. I also have to assist you in hunting down the strigoi and round them up for Mei. Not necessarily in that order, and I was technically already doing both."

"And the third?" I asked, as wary as Death.

"To be determined after I complete the first two."

I groaned. I didn't like the sound of that.

Aurora glanced at me and then my boss, concern etched in her face as well. "What happens if you fail?" she asked Andy.

"Fail?" He snorted but his confidence seemed to vanish as he shifted his weight. "Not in my vocabulary."

Glass snapped and Killion appeared with Katarina's body, his face stone cold and emotionless. He'd shut down, and didn't even show a flicker of relief at seeing Andy and Ghost alive.

I rushed to his side, walking with him as he carried her form past the others. Her face and hands were bloody from dozens of gashes, her clothes torn. There was a sizable wound in her chest, and rather than glass, a shard of wood had pierced it. "Oh no," I murmured. "Not her, too."

He said nothing and kept walking to a clearing several yards away. Using magic, he caused the debris to be swept to the side by an invisible breeze.

"Don't do it, Reveux," Death called.

I glanced at Killion, back to Death. "Do what?"

The master vampire laid her body on the ground so gently, it nearly broke my heart. "Removing the stake won't be enough this time to revive her, even if I give her my blood. Her injuries are too extensive. She took the blast full on." His eyes, black now, locked on mine. "If you share *yours*, she will definitely survive."

A statement, but also a question.

"Chloe," Death yelled, "remember our deal."

If I save her, he could kill you, I reminded Killion.

He nodded. *And that will end you, Grim Zero's vessel. Do you really believe he would do that?*

I honestly wasn't sure. If I perished, that would keep her in her cage a while longer. My contract wasn't up yet, but my deals with Death, as well as SMG, had become convoluted. Right now, I wasn't sure who had the upper hand.

You must be willing of your own accord, Chloe. I will

not ask it of you, if you are unsure about performing such an act.

Like I could deny him anything. And, of course, I wanted to save Katarina. *Shut up and let me think.*

He quirked a brow but said nothing more.

She'd been my friend, albeit an unusual one. She'd helped me out of a lot of jams, offered to kill people for me, beat the stuffing out of me in order to make me faster, better, stronger.

A tug-of-war ensued in my head. I refused to bring harm to Killion, regardless of our connection and my probable subsequent death, if I violated my deal. I wasn't afraid of dying, only of ending his life prematurely with a rash decision.

Katarina didn't have much time. Death marched toward us and Killion tensed.

That morning's events replayed in my head. An idea took hold. *You drank from me just this morning, as I recall.*

The master vampire stilled even more than usual. I hoped he understood my meaning without me coming right out and saying it. I couldn't even afford to think it and take the chance that Death was eavesdropping in my head.

I worked at protecting my telepathy with Killion, but was never sure how much my boss might pick up, thanks to his connection to Grim Zero.

Verbally, I said, "I can't do it. I'm sorry. It's too risky."

Death pulled up, staying a few feet away.

Killion narrowed his eyes, then said, "Fine." Yanking the wood spear from her chest, he cast it away, then raised a hand and a sliver of glass flew into his grip. He cut his wrist in a swift motion and let his blood, infused with my magic, drip into Katarina's open lips. "She is mine to protect and care for." He glanced at Death, a silent warning, even as he said to me, "Not yours."

I held my breath. Would it work? If it did, and Death realized my ruse, would Killion be on his kill list again?

"You'll pay for defying me," Death said, the timbre in his tone making me shiver.

Aurora, Andy, and Ghost formed a half circle around us. Aurora created a ball of witch light to illuminate the scene. It glowed a fuzzy green, reflected in the hundreds of pieces of glass nearby.

At first nothing changed, then Katarina's mouth trembled. Several of her fingers flexed. One eyelid popped open, then the other.

"Katarina," Killion said, smiling down at her.

"What...happened?" she asked, groggily.

"A lot." The two of us assisted her to sit up, then he held his wrist to her, letting her latch on. "We'll explain later."

Death glared and I cleared my throat, shifting to block them as best as I could. "The strigoi did this." I motioned at the destruction. Ghost was normal size again and she danced at my feet. I lifted her to keep her from cutting her paws on the slivers in the grass. "They nearly succeeded at taking out all of us and they still possess my scythe. Find them." I ordered, channeling Grim Zero. "And I will end them."

"I'm not your bloodhound." He seemed unimpressed

with my authority. "Need I remind you that you have equally weighty matters to attend to at SMG."

My legs trembled with exhaustion and my vision swam. I needed to eat and sleep. "Agreed, and I will handle them after I recharge." *And consume my weight in food.* My heart pinged, remembering my favorite cook was no longer feeding me. "Here's the deal."

Death raised a beefy mitt to stop me. "We return to SMG and you take care of Stormfinger. In the morning, you hunt down and harvest the strigoi."

I continued as if he hadn't spoken. "I need to refuel. Like, a huge amount of food, or my magic is going to spin out. I need my personal chef back. Now."

"Forget it." He reached to grab me and I jerked away. "I'm not kidding." I planted my feet, placing myself a decent distance out of his reach. "Let me resurrect Pennyworth, recharge my magic, and formulate a plan for handling both our problems. I can't think right now, much less function. I'm literally tapped out, and when I get overly tired and hungry, guess who finds it easier to come out to play?"

He was an expert at hiding his emotions, and although nothing changed in his expression, I sensed him internally flinch. He hadn't been simply playing to Grim Zero's ego by telling her she had always been more powerful than he was—he'd meant it. Setting her loose in the world was his worst nightmare. "You fail at crossing over the archimagus, or recovering the scythe, and I will take his"—he pointed at Killion—"Undead life again." He jutted his chin at Katarina. "Along with his minion."

Katarina and Killion stepped up, closing rank around

me. I knew they were about to engage in an argument over his threat, so I stuck out my hand. "Deal. Failure isn't in my lexicon." I winked cheekily at Andy.

Death ignored my outstretched hand. "I know what you did, Chloe."

I played dumb, but when he vanished into thin air, I released the breath I'd been holding.

"What did that mean?" Katarina asked.

"Nothing," I said. Death hadn't been fooled by my acting job, and his threat laid heavy on me. "How do you feel?"

"Like I could raise the dead." She chuckled when my face fell and threw an arm around my shoulders. "Don't worry. It will be our little secret."

NINETEEN

Although we scoured the remnants of the arboretum, we found no evidence of Prince Oz. I prayed he'd somehow escaped and would find his cousin.

Pennyworth greeted us the instant we walked into Killion's penthouse. He bowed deeply to me. "I knew you were special the moment Killion brought you here, but I never imagined the twists and turns my life would take because of you."

I could smell the feast he'd prepared, my mouth salivating. I took hold of his arm and forced his lowered gaze up to meet mine. "I couldn't be more sorry about what happened. I hope we can still be friends."

He patted my hand. "Water under the bridge. I hope you're hungry."

Wasn't I always?

Katarina slapped him on the back as she strutted for the dining room and the bounty waiting for us. Aurora and Andy greeted him, and he accepted sloppy kisses from Ghost.

Leaving him and Killion to have a word in private, I dropped into a chair before passing my favorite foods around the table. When everyone's plates were full, we chowed down.

Killion joined us eventually, his face taut, as Pennyworth disappeared into the kitchen. The master vampire's anger was as palatable to me as the dinner I shoveled into my mouth. It simmered under his skin and prickled against my own. I tried to soothe him, but I was still angry as well. What saved me was having these precious moments with my friends. The time for vengeance would come soon enough.

We were halfway through the meal, Pennyworth sitting with us at my request, when a black storm burst through the door without warning.

The vampire moved so fast I didn't have time to come to my feet before his vise-like grip wrapped around my neck and lifted me free of the chair. He pinned me to the wall, breaking a framed picture and slamming the air from my lungs. Between that and the cracking sound of glass, I flashed back to the arboretum and screamed.

His eyes were as dark as his skin and they burned with rage. "If you ever cause harm to my soul mate again," he hissed, spit hitting my cheek, "I will torture you until you beg me to kill you."

Chaos erupted. Pennyworth yelled, "Omwee! Release her at once!"

In the next breath, Killion was on him, breaking his hold and pinning him to the ground.

I had never met Pennyworth's partner, and as Killion restrained him, threatening to end his Undead life once and for all, I rubbed my throat and leaned against the wall. "It's okay." My voice came out hoarse. "He has every right to be upset. I'm sorry, Omwee. I would never intentionally hurt Pennyworth. Killion, please. Enough violence has happened today."

The butler stepped between us as Killion allowed Omwee to stand once more. He didn't release his death grip on him, though. Silent communication passed between Pennyworth and his partner, and the fight drained from Omwee like a balloon losing air. "I apologize," he forced from clenched teeth.

"You are out of line," Killion growled. "I should banish you."

"No banishing." I placed my hand over Killion's that was still at Omwee's throat. "We're all okay."

I felt Killion's internal struggle. I kept my hand on his. *Please. Let him go.*

The moment Killion released him, Omwee stormed out.

"He's never like that." Pennyworth brushed at my clothes, distressed. "My sincerest apologies. I'm all he has and I already explained to him that it was my fault, not yours, but as you can see, he is extremely upset."

I hugged the butler. "It was *not* your fault, and I understand his reaction and"—I shot a look at Killion—"fiercely protective attitude. You deserve nothing less, and I hope I can make it up to him, and you, one of these days."

Pennyworth guided me back to my chair, picking it

up from where it had fallen. "Please don't think poorly of him."

"Not at all. I'm happy he's so committed to you."

Killion was not as easily appeased. "His actions will have consequences. He is never to touch Chloe again."

Pennyworth bowed his head. "Of course, master."

The butler used his magic to restore the glass in the frame and rehang the picture, then disappeared into the kitchen. Everyone was deathly quiet and I shot Killion a chastising glance. He was in no mood for an argument; he was their leader, the one who set the rules for his nest, expected them to follow those rules, and when they stepped over the line, it was his job to discipline them. I didn't always like it, but it wasn't my place to intervene.

The air was tense as we returned to dessert and coffee. Pennyworth cleared our plates once we finished, and then plopped a stack of books on the table near my elbow.

"Know your enemy," he said, sounding like a wise sage. "I dug up more on the strigoi, including ways they can be hunted, captured, and supposedly terminated."

"Supposedly?" Aurora echoed.

"There are a multitude of legends regarding such methods, or at the very least, causing serious injury to slow them down."

I handed the witch a volume with spells and charms specifically for protecting against the superior vampires, and another to Andy on tracking them. "This is awesome, Pennyworth. Thank you."

· · ·

BY THE TIME the sun teased its way above the horizon for a new day, I was fed, had five hours of sleep and had enjoyed a full-body massage courtesy of my soulmate. He'd started at my feet while I read more about our common enemy, then worked his way up. My book was soon forgotten, and everything from my hands, legs, shoulders, and back was intensely and intimately caressed and kissed until I begged for mercy.

It seemed I wasn't the only one grateful that we were alive. Our lovemaking didn't completely assuage his anger, but it took the edge off. All of it cleared my head and refreshed my magic. As I showered, a plan for eliminating the strigoi threat once and for all came to me and I smiled to myself. It was going to be a good day for hunting.

"You seem happy," Killion said, as he joined me and began soaping me up.

I leaned against his broad chest, enjoying the solid feel of him. "What would I have done without Pennyworth? Ghost? Even Andy? You bet I'm happy, and I will make sure nothing happens to them again."

He kissed my head. "*We* will make sure of it."

First, I had to handle Stormfinger. Once I downed breakfast, I sent an email to SMG. *I'm ready*, was all it said.

Three seconds later, Death appeared in the living room. I rose from the sofa, kissed Killion, and gripped Ghost's collar. "We need to make this quick. I have a date with Lasarus and Sable."

Death held out a hand. I took it, and the next

moment I was once more standing in the great hall of Soul Management Group.

TWENTY

"Here's what I need you to do."

Death blinked. "*Me?*"

We walked toward Mei's office, me setting the pace. Ghost trotted alongside, tail wagging. "It wasn't my idea to kill the archimagus with a lightning bolt." Although, it seemed fitting. "If he hasn't crossed and is haunting this place, he needs an apology. Closure over his death." This was Grim 101. "You're going to give it to him. Mei, too."

He snorted. "That's not happening."

Figured that he would make this harder than it had to be. "We are dealing with an advanced magic user, but he's still human. *Was* human. He had plans and dreams. Wacko ones, but still. He even had a woman he loved." I thought of Pennyworth and Omwee. Aurora and Andy. Me and Killion. For a moment, I felt bad for Death. Had he loved Grim Zero? Whether he had or not, I couldn't imagine being immortal and not having someone to share with. "He has unfinished business and we need to help him with that."

Death brimmed with impatience. "He got what he deserved. I'm surprised you would defend him, since you're all about justice."

"In his mind it wasn't wrong or evil. You have to put yourself in his shoes and think like him. Know your enemy and all that."

"Tell me you're not quoting *Art of War* to me. If so, it reads, 'If you know the enemy and know yourself—'"

"Let me stop you right there. I'm not quoting anything, it's just good strategy."

"Okay." He sounded unconvinced. We stopped when we reached the door of the office. "What is it you think I can do?"

"Engage him in an honest discussion about what happened. Put the blame for his electrifying exit on God or whoever made the call. We need him to believe that a higher power ended his human existence because he *was* out of line. Take the heat off us and use the Law of Karma to justify what happened. Also, it wouldn't hurt if I knew who might be waiting for him on the other side."

"Waiting?"

"A loved one. A beloved pet. We need a carrot to dangle."

Death thought it over. "I'll see what I can find out."

"Don't—" He disappeared. "Leave," I finished, now speaking to thin air.

Mei was AWOL. Not that I expected her to be present for the event, but it would have been nice. Her office was restored to its former glory, the mountain view intact. I took a moment to appreciate it.

"Neymar?" I used his first name, hoping to establish rapport. "I'm sorry about what they did to you." I certainly wasn't above throwing others under the bus, in this case. I had a job to do, and I intended to get this done and get out. The strigoi would be harder and take more time. "I had no idea The Big Guy was going to strike you down with lightning."

Ghost perked her ears and raised her nose into the air. A chilly breeze slapped my face and a milky gray ghost zoomed past. I could hear the hate in Stormfinger's voice when he said, "You were just doing your job, right, Grave Girl?"

I followed his form as it faded and had a new idea. Using the Law of Karma might aggravate him, but... "Your contract was up, you know." Not technically true, but he didn't know that. "There was nothing to be done about it. Your soul agreed to go out at that time, and you have to admit, it was a spectacular exit. The magical community is still abuzz about it."

I thought I'd lost him when he didn't respond. Then, "They're talking about me?"

Ah, the ego. Appealing to it worked pretty well.

His form zoomed by again. Ghost barked. This must have seemed like a cool game to her, especially when he kept moving. He did it hoping I couldn't touch him with my scythe. He apparently hadn't realized I was without it.

I whispered a command in Ghost's ear. She lay down, looking as if she were asleep. Moss' trick had come in handy. Stormfinger's flying around sent the lovely smells of clear mountain air and a hint of cedar and pine at me. "Your acolyte, Sokoloff, is memorializing you around town."

"He is?"

I pulled out Mei's chair and made myself comfortable. What was it like, I wondered, being in charge of souls? "You can head back to the earthly plane and verify it." At least that would get him out of SMG. Then Aurora and Killion could help me trap him long enough to use my tools to cross him forcefully. "I bet he'd love you to visit."

He buffed the back of my head, sending a lock of my hair flipping to the other side. "Do you think I'm stupid?"

"Not in the least." Although he was acting like a two-year-old having a tantrum.

He flew at me again. The door cracked open at the same moment Ghost jumped to her feet and morphed. The psychopomp leaped into the air and caught Stormfinger by his arm as he reached to strike me again.

His face turned startled; Mei and Death's did as well, watching as Ghost and the archimagus made a popping noise and disappeared.

"There," I said, coming to my feet and clapping my hands together. "One earthbound spirit crossed to the wonderful afterlife."

Mei's tight shoulders dipped with relief. She hustled toward the desk, shooing me out of her way. "Finally." She took her seat and scooted the chair in. "Take her back to earth."

That was it? "Thank you would be the appropriate

response." I towered several inches over her and leaned closer, trying to snag her gaze. "Along with that, I want Death's full cooperation and help with handling the strigoi. Andy is a decent tracker, but I need the best."

When she deigned to look at me, her gaze could have melted a polar ice cap. "Next time we bring Grim Zero back"—she was once again addressing Death, rather than me—"make sure it's in a more likable vessel."

My magic went haywire, channeling my alter ego. I felt smug satisfaction when she twitched slightly from the punch of it. "Be careful." I lowered my voice to Grim Zero's dangerous purr. "Or I'll make Stormfinger's destruction of your office look like child's play. I'll gather every earthbound soul I can find and deliver them right here."

Ghost popped back in, panting and ready for more. I petted her head and marched to the exit, motioning for Death to follow. "Come on, boss. We have two lousy vampires to take care of."

I sensed him hesitate and then heard Mei say with resignation, "Don't come back until it's handled."

Exiting, I smiled to myself, my footsteps echoing confidently in the great hall. Ghost bounced on the balls of her feet by my side.

"I hate you," Death snarled when he caught up with us.

I punched his massive bicep. "You love me and you know it."

He grabbed my hand and we dissolved into dust.

TWENTY-ONE

Twilight hung in the air, everything still and steeped in shadows. "Why is it dark?" I asked, looking around at the place we'd landed. I swallowed my queasiness. "Where are we?"

Death began walking across a field of wildflowers. "Time moves differently here than on the earthly plane."

That did nothing for my shaky stomach. "Where's Ghost?"

"I sent her back to Earth."

I ran to catch up with him. "Exactly which plane are we on?" Killion and Andy were waiting for me. "I thought we were hunting the strigoi."

"We're searching for your scythe. Once you're in possession of that, you can find the Undead wankers."

His accent was heavy again. He had something up his sleeve. "You didn't answer my question. Where are we?"

"The realm of the Fae."

I stopped. "The *what*?"

He continued on, undaunted and seemingly uninterested in explaining himself.

"Wait." I grabbed his arm. "Why are we here? The Fae don't have my blade."

He flexed his huge bicep and broke my grip. The tall wildflowers parted in his wake. "When we were on DuMort Hill, I could sense the scythe, but it was indistinct, its normal vibration muted."

I sent a soft ripple of magic flowing over the land, not sure what to expect. The flowers did not move aside for me. In fact, they reached for me, tangling around my legs, their scent filling my nostrils and making me sneeze.

Great, just what I needed—an allergy attack. "I don't follow."

He scanned the horizon. "It was as if it was there, yet not. As though it existed in the same location, only a different dimension."

I took in the rolling landscape. "Why would the strigoi hide it in this one? How *could* they? They can't come and go from this realm, can they?"

Finally, he came to a halt and put his hands on his hips. "Nope, they can't."

I was still confused. "Then how did it get here? It's not like Oz..." I stopped. "You think the Fae prince is in cahoots with them. But he said they kidnapped his cousin."

"Mmm hmm." He turned left and started walking again. "That's what he said."

He obviously didn't believe him. *Kill?* There was no response from the blade. "I thought the Fae couldn't lie."

A slight shrug. "Doesn't it seem odd that he was at

the bar the night Lasarus rolled in and confronted Killion? Then again at the arboretum last night when the explosion occurred? After that shifter betrayed you, I'd think you'd be more suspicious about the good prince's intentions."

"You're drawing conclusions with no proof. Why would you suspect his involvement when it comes to my scythe? You think he's working with Lasarus?"

He glanced at me, eyes snapping. "Don't you?"

"Why would he? The strigoi kidnapped his cousin!"

"So he claims."

Unwinding a particularly eager sunflower from around my thigh, I shook my head and turned down my magic to stop the plants from strangling me. "Walk me through this. Oz and his cousin venture into our realm, we suspect they're responsible for the dried up husks of people we found at the arboretum, but they aren't; the strigoi are. Sable steals my scythe. Oz claims they kidnapped Harmony and was told to meet Sable and Lasarus at the arboretum. It's a trap, meant to kill all of us." He nods. I continue. "Still not finding the connecting dot where Oz is in league with Lasarus and my scythe is here in Fae-land. You're grasping at straws."

In true Death fashion, he glared. "I keep thinking that one of these days the brain cells in your head will actually fire."

I gave him an impolite gesture. "You are the rudest person I've ever met."

He sighed dramatically. "Lasarus may have forced Oz to hide the scythe here in exchange for Harmony."

"Oh." I may have regretted flipping him off a *teensy* bit. "And now Oz is dead."

"There was no body."

"Can't you check with Mei and find out if the prince is among the recently departed?"

"Their souls are handled differently. Universal Laws don't govern this world like they do the human one."

Had this been covered in the manual? I scanned my memory. "SMG has no power over them?"

"They often live to be a thousand years old, some more. They have an afterlife, but this plane has its own conventions. We don't interfere."

"A thousand years?" Yikes. I studied my boss, knowing he was even older. "Except we're here because this is a special case. Can you sense Kill? I feel...something. Not sure what, but the blade isn't responding to my call, so I don't think it's him." Her? It? Did the scythe have a preference? "Will the Fae be happy to see us?"

As if in answer, hundreds of glowing eyes lit the night, peeking from between bushes and trees.

"Not exactly," Death replied. "We're violating the sacred pact between them and SMG."

A chittering noise went up and the vegetation that had been so eager to touch me began to slink away, creating a wide path. "You always know how to show me a good time. What will they do to us?"

He stalked forward, following the walkway the wild-flowers created. "Kill us if they can."

Awesome. The eyes seemed to get closer. I hurried to reach him; he was the only means I had to get out of here.

A rip appeared in the landscape directly in front of

us, making him pull up abruptly. I slammed into his back, ricocheted, and lost my footing. My butt hit the ground and the chittering turned to laughter.

From the rip appeared soldiers, stepping through it like a doorway. In their midst a man cloaked in richly dyed purple robes and a crown waited. His white hair hung long over his shoulders, accentuating sharp cheekbones and perfect skin. Piercing violet eyes, like Killion's, sized us up.

"King Huvino," Death said with a nod, as I scrambled to my feet. "Pardon our intrusion."

The king lifted his chin, and although he was a good six inches shorter than my boss, had no trouble looking down his nose. He sniffed and the perfect face turned sour. "You do not belong here."

"We don't." Death appeared completely at ease, while my heart hammered like a bass drum in my chest. The guards were poised and ready to strike, and I had no scythe or psychopomp. The tools probably wouldn't do me a bit of good anyway. Death motioned at me. "Neither does her scythe, the one you hide within your realm."

Huvino didn't even glance my way. "We have no death blade here."

My feet were rooted to the spot and the gathering around us of Fae creatures kept my pulse skipping. Their magic was so different than mine, Death's, even Aurora's. It was sweet and delicate, yet seemed to conceal shark teeth below the surface.

Thin streams of it tickled mine, inviting me to play. Even as I kept mine locked down, I sensed the flora we stood knee-deep in creeping toward my legs once more. Not to simply enjoy my life-giving abilities, but to suck me dry.

The corpses we'd found... had they been killed by the Fae or the strigoi? Both?

"Maybe he's right," I murmured to Death, shifting uncomfortably. Katarina had taught me how to stay aware of multiple adversaries when surrounded, and how to pick an order in which to take out the first, second, third, and so on. I saw no weaker link here. "We should go."

Death ignored me, casual as could be. "Prince Oz is dabbling in things he shouldn't be. He's upsetting the balance between our world and yours. I have a duty to remove the scythe from this one and return it to mine."

The king snorted, and even that was elegant, his aristocratic nose still high. "He is no prince to us. He and my daughter were banished some time ago. He may not enter our dimension, and so, if he *is* the culprit who possesses the grim blade, you will not find it here."

Death brushed his jaw with his knuckles. "Banished for what?"

I was curious, too. At that moment, however, all I could focus on was fighting off the tendrils of magic weaving themselves around me. They were as prolific as the glowers doing the same. Vines encircled my ankles, my calves. "Um, boss?" They began to tighten. "It's definitely time to leave."

"You won't mind if we have a look around, will you?" Death kept an observant eye on the king. "Perhaps Oz gave the blade to a friend who is storing it here, mate."

His tone suggested Huvino, himself, might be in on the charade. That didn't seem wise, but I forgot the vines, up to my thighs now, and their magical counterparts, as I sized up our host with a more critical eye. "We've gotten off on the wrong foot. I'm Chloe, by the way. It would be in your best interest to help us." Everything paused—the vines, the king, his subjects. While Death held sway with most beings out of fear, I seemed to invite cooperation. It was the Chloe in me, my true essence. I wanted everyone to get along. "We have no interest in interfering with your realm, only in retrieving what is rightfully mine. If the prince is at odds with you as well as us, we are allies, not enemies. We'll leave you be and owe you a favor if you assist us."

Death's brows dipped when he sent an over-the-shoulder glare my way. Then he smoothed out his features before facing Huvino once more. "She's right—all we want is the blade. Help us and *she'll* owe you a favor."

I stood still, keeping my face open and calm. Killion would be proud—not a hint of fear or unease shone in my features or scented my magic.

"You are a very unusual creature," the king said, stepping toward me. His guards remained ready to defend. He glanced at the vines winding around my legs. They tickled my hips as they rose higher. "The smell of your power is...enticing."

Death stiffened. The king placed himself face-to-face with me. It wasn't even nose-to-nose, since Huvino was shorter than me. He kept that haughty air, though, studying me with curiosity.

I longed to correct his terms, however, at that moment, it seemed unwise to provoke the king.

That was until I felt his magic prod mine. Probing. Seeking. Trying to lock in on it.

For what? To understand it, and me, better. But it was rude and intrusive—more so than his followers doing it—because of his absolute and incredible power.

My skin flushed with a sudden invisible rash, as if he were peeling it away from my body, seeking the layers underneath. I wasn't about to play nice if he was going to step over that particular boundary. "Stop it."

My tone held a dire warning, yet he didn't so much as pause, his invasive magic a finger stabbing me.

"I said, *stop*."

The king lifted a thick brow, as if silently asking, "Or what?"

Reading my mind, Death made tiny "no" motions with his head. Without thought or hesitation, I sent a huge pulse of magic at Huvino.

He wasn't expecting it, or perhaps not anticipating it would be so forceful. It lifted him off his pointy-shoed feet, slamming him backwards. He landed flat on the ground with a yelp.

"Or that," I said with a grin.

Instantly, he was helped up and I was surrounded. Death rolled his eyes. *You just couldn't resist, could you?*

The king brushed dirt and grass from his cape and knocked the hands away of the overly helpful guards. "How dare you!"

Death's magic wrapped around me like armor. I eyed those barricading me from Huvino and wondered why they thought I wouldn't do the same to them. "I asked you to stop," I said to the king. "Didn't your mother teach you that probing others without consent is just plain wrong?"

Hesitating, he studied me with those violet eyes again. Something in my words seemed to have registered and his face fell. "My mother went into The Fade centuries ago. She was..." He shook his head, as if the action might shake off an old memory. His lips trembled with a smile he tried to keep from them. "You remind me of her."

Okay, that was *not* what I'd expected. "I'm sorry about her death. I lost mine, too. That's a hole that no one else can ever fill."

His nose lowered from its lofty perch. "I think I like you."

I couldn't say the same. "I thought the Fae were immortal."

"Immortal as the other living things you see here. When we fade, we turn back into the elements of nature. We might become a tree,"—he pointed to the nearby grove of them—"or a flower. Water or air. There are no bodies buried here. We transition from one entity to another instantly."

Jeez, I hoped I wasn't standing on his mother.

"It is the same for humans," he continued. "Only we live longer in these physical forms because there is no disease or illness here. Your transition takes longer, especially since you delay it by attempting to preserve the dead."

"I do apologize that we've imposed, but I'd appreciate

it if you'd help me out. Is the whereabouts of my scythe known to you?"

"If I tell you, you will owe me a favor of my choosing at a time of my choosing."

Yeah, no. "I agree to a favor. If you're instrumental in helping me recover the scythe, and your return request is mutually agreeable and fits my time schedule, we have a deal."

"What is time? You mortals are always so worried about trivial things." He waited for me to argue; I didn't. He gave me a tight smile. "Are you creating a faery bargain with me, Chloe?"

Death sent a warning glance over the king's shoulder.

"I'm offering a grim reaper pledge." That wasn't actually a thing, but it sounded good. "Simple, straightforward, no hidden agenda. Take it or leave it."

A pause. His followers seemed to hold their breath. I thought he was about to agree when he shook his head. "I see no reason to say yes. What could I possibly want from a grim?"

"I'm a very *unusual creature*," I reminded him. "And I know you're itching to probe me again."

Death looked like he might throw up. "Chloe." My name sounded like an omen on his lips. "We need to go."

The flowering vines still held me in place. I shot him a quizzical glance. Did he want the scythe or not? "If you're as powerful as you seem," I said to Huvino, "then we could do a lot together for our realms, but we must be truthful with each other for our partnership to work."

I gave him my best smile. *Come on, big boy. I want my scythe back.*

He wasn't wowed by the smile or my words. "You entered my realm without permission." He didn't throw my exact phrasing back at me, but close. "A violation of our rules. Death may leave." He glanced at my boss and the guards faced him, keeping a blockade in front of me. "But you," he said, and I felt the vines cut into my skin, "never will."

TWENTY-TWO

I chuckled even though my stomach clenched. "No can do, your highness. My world is one of death; I don't fit in here, as you've so generously pointed out."

My eyes locked with Death's and he nodded. Before the guards, or anyone else, could move, we reached for each other.

Too late. I was already stuck in place, but now, he was too. Our fingers stayed inches apart.

I sent my reaper magic into the slithering clamps around my calves and thighs. As expected, the jolt shocked them enough to ease their hold on me. Problem was, Death was still locked down.

I strained for his hand, ignoring the yells of the guards, the cries of the other Fae, and the King's roar of anger. While the vines loosened, there was still a barricade of guards between us.

We clamored to attain the connection we needed,

and our fingertips nearly brushed. A guard knocked the butt of his spear into my arm, sending my hand flying in the opposite direction.

Equally frustrated, scared, and infuriated, my magic rammed him and rushed out in all directions. The guards toppled, trees snapped in half. The tidal wave crushed the flowers in the field, flattening all in its path.

As Death smirked and I grasped his hand, I saw the king's eyes once more alight with curiosity. What did he think of my unusual creature status now?

I didn't have time to worry about it as I was transported through time, space, and dimensions. A sudden tug took hold in my chest. *Kill.* My hand instinctively shot out as we were reforming, and the next thing I knew, we landed on DuMort Hill.

My hand smacked hard on the ground, my knees slamming into the dead soil. The impact jarred me head to toe.

It was late afternoon here, the sun on my left. I wasn't always accurate at directions, but having been here before and knowing the location of the arboretum from this point, I could guess.

My palm itched, as Death said, "What the devil are we doing here? I aimed for the penthouse."

"It's Kill." I closed my eyes and tested the earth under my hand with a thread of magic. "I felt him. When we disapparated. It sucked us here. You were right about the location. My blade is below us."

"There's nothing but dirt and clay." He shaded his eyes from the sun and turned in a circle, staring at the barren wasteland. "We already determined it hasn't been disturbed by a burial."

My phone buzzed, now working again that we were in the earthly plane. In a way, it was a welcome relief. "Magic?" I guessed. It was usually a fair explanation.

He shrugged. "I don't see or feel any residuals from it. You?"

"No," I admitted. The call was from Killion. "Hey," I answered, digging my heel into the place my hand had landed. The ground was so hard, it barely made a scratch.

"Are you all right? You've been gone a long while and our connection was dark."

"You can check Stormfinger off today's to-do list. Still working on retrieving the blade."

There was a pregnant pause. "You're needed at the clinic. Dr. O'Leary has come down with a virus. I have asked Harlow to step in and see what she can do, but she is not a veterinarian, you understand."

A vampire could heal a great deal of injuries, and perhaps even cure certain diseases, but the thought of her running the place sent chills through me. Some of the animals, and possibly their owners, would pick up on her predatory nature and reject any attempts to help them. "Please tell me she's retracted her fangs. If she frightens off Patty, I'm screwed."

"The office manager is still employed, rest assured, and Harlow has found she likes the work, although she implores you to return as soon as possible. While she can relieve pain and successfully treat minor cases, her presence has raised questions with Dr. Banks."

I bet. JR had no idea about me and my "friends," but

even mundanes could sense the innate danger from supernaturals. Not that she would hurt him, but vampires were naturally threatening in general. Squeezing my eyes shut, I pinched the bridge of my nose. "How's Ghost?"

Another of those pauses. This one made me open my eyes, my gut suddenly tight. "Isn't she with you?"

"Death sent her back here to you, I assumed."

Death, hearing the stress in my voice, faced me. "What is it?"

Killion went on alert. "I haven't seen her."

I lowered the phone and stalked to my boss. "Where is she? What did you do with her?"

He frowned. "Who?"

"Ghost!" I nearly punched him. "She's not at Killion's."

"But that's where I..." He got that nauseated look again. "Bloody hell."

I thought I might explode. "What?"

He started marching off. "You stay here and hunt for the blade. Have the toothy wonder come help. The shifter, too. I'll go get her."

"Get her from—"

"Be right back," he said over my words and disappeared.

I raised the device, wishing I could throw it at him. "Did you hear that, Toothy Wonder?"

Killion growled. "He and I are going to have a talk."

Pretty sure I didn't want to be around for that. "I'm at DuMort Hill."

"I'll be there shortly."

We disconnected. I heard footsteps and my stomach fell. Slowly, I turned, and yep. Not good.

Sable and Lasarus carried black metal batons that resembled flashlights. "Death should have ended us when he had the chance," Lasarus said with a savage grin.

"He should have." I tried to keep a neutral face; I didn't want them to see how unnerved I was being here in the middle of nowhere with them. No scythe, no psychopomp, and nothing I could use for a weapon. I didn't even have an animal or shifter whose mind I could control. Stalling seemed a good idea—maybe Killion would get here in time to help end this charade. "He'll be back in a minute to finish the job. You should hang around and wait."

Sable stopped in front of me, tapping the baton in the palm of her hand. "You're hard to get rid of."

"I could say the same about you. The explosion was a nice try."

"Bad pennies, and all that." She tilted her head and scanned me, her tongue licking at the piercing in her lip. "I have plenty more torture techniques to use on you."

I could see the serial killer in her eyes. I almost wished I was back with the king of the Fae. *Stall.* "You buried my blade?"

Lasarus casually examined his nails. He'd sharpened them into claws. "Not exactly."

I pointed at the ground. "I sense it. How did you get it under there without leaving a trace? Must be some unusual magic."

He thumped his baton against his leg...once, twice. "*Unique* is a better term for it. Like the Fae king, I'm a collector. I like rare magical artifacts. On occasion, those happen to be supernaturals like you."

A collector? Death hadn't mentioned anything about that. "You mean like Professor Slughorn?"

The baton stopped. "Who?"

"No one ever gets my Harry Potter references," I grumbled. "It's like you all live in a cave." I worked through in my head who I would take out first. "Artifacts, huh? What type? How big is your collection? Small, I'm guessing." I sent a look toward his lower half, insinuating something entirely different.

He grinned, cocky and ruthless. "You'll find out soon enough."

I can hardly wait. "You know Huvino?"

Oz appeared out of thin air at that moment and Death's earlier suspicions smacked me in the face. "He knows me," the prince stated.

The Fae's betrayal didn't sting as much as Pepper's. I still wanted to strip his magic and torture him—so *not* a Chloe reaction. "You're alive. Nice fake. You knew there was a bomb, didn't you? You set us up."

"He has my cousin. I wasn't lying about that."

"Where's my blade?"

"What, no threats?" Lasarus taunted. Sable strolled behind me, playing with her baton. "No further small talk to buy time until Lord Killion gets here to rescue you?"

I tried to keep Sable in my sights, but if I turned to do so, I'd lose the males. Three on one wasn't the best odds, but I was suddenly glad once again that I'd had Katarina as a teacher. She loved to throw multiple assailants at me during training. "You really have a hard-on for him, don't you? I mentioned this before, but I guess you're pretty old and have memory issues. I don't need to be rescued."

He opened his mouth to reply and I launched myself at the weakest link in the threesome—Prince Oz.

TWENTY-THREE

The prince didn't react fast enough and I flattened him. At least, that's what I surmised until he murmured in my ear as he gently wrestled with me, "Let me help you."

It was said so softly I almost didn't pick it up around the yelling and grunting he did as he flailed dramatically. Was he playing both sides of the coin? Should I trust him?

Either way, I was pissed about his betrayal. "I'm calling in my favor," I hissed and landed a right hook to his jaw, a fleeting sense of satisfaction flooding me when blood flew from his mouth. Whether or not the blow caused him true distress, he looked like a prizefighter down for the count. I used the distraction to kick out a foot and nail Sable in the ankle. She cried, swinging her baton wildly at my head as her bone broke and she crumpled to the dry ground.

Lasarus jumped me, his baton crackling with electrical current. I shifted right when he tried to jab me with it, and hauled Oz into a sitting position to block the next stab.

I let go and the end of the weapon hit the Fae prince in his left pec, right over his heart. He went rigid, jerking from the high level voltage. While he might be my enemy, I still said, "Sorry," as I jumped to my feet and booted Lasarus in the arm.

The heat of the fight coursed through my veins. Like the vampire who'd trained me, I felt a sureness inside of me, the surge of animalistic delight. The strigoi and Fae hadn't learned or accepted the truth yet—I was top predator in this war.

Even as Lasarus recoiled and Oz tipped over, immobile, I calculated my next move. And the next. After my last encounters with Sable and Lasarus, I knew their tells. Being trained by Katarina, I'd automatically logged their go-to moves and noted where they left themselves vulnerable.

I punched, whirled, jumped, and kicked. I used them against each other, reveling in my speed and strength. I wasn't only fighting for myself, I was fighting for Killion. For Aurora and Andy. Even for Ghost.

What had happened to her? Where was Death?

I couldn't let myself think about them. I had to stay focused on the battle in front of me.

Dirt covered my hands, my face, my clothes. The others fared no better. At one point, as Lasarus once again tried to stun me into submission, I saw Oz trip him. The strigoi turned the weapon on the prince, this time catching him upside the temple with the barrel.

Oz was out like a light. Sable had gone full monster,

losing her clothes and gaining rows of shark-like teeth and claws the size of steak knives. Fending off a blow from Lasarus, I lunged left when I should have went right and she caught me with one of those claws, slicing through my belly.

I staggered, the deep gashes spurting blood like a geyser. She laughed, or more accurately, her beast did, the sound grating over me like a thousand slashes of icy sleet. "Die, bitch," she growled through that mouthful of teeth.

"Not yet." Lasarus shoved his weight into me and knocked me down. I tried to fight but the searing pain across my abdomen made me slow. The lacerations burned. A massive hand wrapped around my throat and squeezed. My vision blurred, cleared, blurred again. I couldn't breathe. Warm blood soaked my clothes and stuck to my skin. "We need her to get him."

Killion. I had to protect him. They wouldn't kill me. Not yet. And that meant I could muster up a fresh fight once my wounds healed. If I could keep him away, I could...

My brain went fuzzy. The burning spread. That's when I remembered Sable's claws were tipped with that dreadful venom.

"That's right," she said, holding up one set of claws and clicking them together. Green gel oozed down her hand and onto her forearm. "It's paralyzing and often lethal, depending on how much magic I put in it. My specialty."

Strigoi themselves were unique in the world of the Undead. One with venom, I guessed, even more so.

Lasarus was a collector, all right. She was one of his artifacts.

The world grew hazy, the edges dark. The burning spread and left a scary numbness in its place. Sable's laughter echoed in my ears as Lasarus stared at me. "You are the most valuable addition to my collection to date," he said with a delighted grin. I didn't miss Sable's eye roll. "Too bad I have to kill you."

He used a finger to pull a strand of hair from my face, almost caressingly. His disgusting breath made me queasy; my situation even more so. I tried to spit in his eye but my mouth was dry, my tongue now numb.

As if he could read my thoughts, he patted my cheek and made clucking noises. "There, there, don't worry. I promise I'll make it last. Once Killion joins the party, we'll get started for real. That way,"—he booped the end of my nose—"he can enjoy the torture twice as much. He'll watch you suffer, and at the same time, he'll feel it as well."

Sadist. With all my effort, I tried to send out a pulse of magic. Warn Killion. Call Death. Anything. I could barely breathe, however, and I couldn't make a sound, my vocal cords now useless. Desperate, I reached for Grim Zero, begging for her help.

Only a stark emptiness greeted me. Panicking, I toppled the barrier, calling to her. *Help!*

She didn't respond. Wherever she had retreated to, either she couldn't hear my nine-one-one or she couldn't respond.

Had Sable's venom affected her, too?

Barreling down into the magic she always had, I

focused on finding it, finding her. As I sank into it, searching for the power I could unleash, I felt a new sensation take hold.

My alter ago grabbed me, but she didn't infuse me with her power. She pushed me under the waters of hers.

Everything went inky black, then grew even darker, much like being plunged into the center of the earth where no light ever touched. Suffocating.

I struggled against it, now fighting an internal battle. *Don't do this*, I pleaded. *I need you.*

She pushed me deeper. The world spun out, her power a cavern of death and rebirth, over and over. Billions of creatures since the beginning of time, all connected to her.

And all now aware of me.

The weight of it was too much. It tore me apart, even as it crushed me under it. With one last thought of Killion, my forever soulmate, I kicked for the surface, only to be yanked back into the abyss by those billions of souls.

Stop fighting, she purred. The words reverberated in my blood, my bones, my cells. *Let go.*

There was nothing left inside me, no matter how hard I tried to focus my magic or tap into hers. The fight, the wildness, all of it, was just gone.

I'll never give up, I swore to her, but even as I thought the words, my soul winked out.

I CAME to in a pain-filled blur. My eyelids were boulders, my arms secured above my head, tingling from lack of blood flow. Mouth dry as the dirt on DuMort Hill, I moaned through cracked lips and my aching body swung lazily, suspended in air.

My magic reached out, searching for life. Wherever I was, there was none present, only the bones of the long-dead. The place had a type of sentience that hung thick in the darkness, wrapping itself around me and calling to my spirit. Even the scent of it was...lifeless. Dry. Barren.

Swimming in a haze of pain, I barely noticed the ghosts fading in and out of my awareness. The gloom was so thick, I could not see anything but their flickering energy.

My consciousness seemed to do the same, like a cork bobbing up to float on the sea, only to be shoved down again into its murky depths. Each time I came to the surface, I felt more confused about how much time had passed. Hours? Days? Longer?

I shivered hard, over and over, struggling to remember who I was, figure out why I was here. Forcing myself to stay conscious, I licked my dry lips and tried to form words. At first, nothing came out, my tongue sticking to the roof of my mouth. After several more attempts, I managed to call out, "Hello?" I swallowed hard, listening to the word echo, as if I were in a cavern. My left rib hurt with every breath, my abdomen complaining. "Is anyone...there?"

The darkness did not answer. The bones in the place stirred.

My eyes were swollen and keeping them open was too much work. The simple effort to call out had exhausted me and I slipped into unconsciousness again.

The next time I woke, my gaze snagged on a faint glow in the distance; it flickered like candlelight. The barely-there illumination at least allowed me to register my surroundings—heavily shadowed stone walls, an archway, a tunnel. There seemed to be coves on either side of the passage. Barely there movement caught my eye.

A small body skittered along the edge of the wall, the rat pausing for a moment to lift its head. Whiskers twitching, it sniffed the air.

I caught the metallic tang it had. Blood. A glance down showed a pool of it beneath my dangling feet.

As I noticed my ripped and tattered shirt, the previous events came back in a wavy haze. Sable and her claws. Lasarus and his baton. Oz and his betrayal.

I groaned and the act cost me. The skin over my wounds had partially healed, yet the poison stilled coursed through my system. The odor of it was in my veins and the rat eyed me with suspicion.

Every small undertaking caused me to sway. The dull clink of chains told me my manacles were metal, thick and solid. No taking command of the vermin's mind and using it to chew through them.

As if sensing my attention on it, the rat lowered its nose to the stones once more and scurried on. It had a rather odd patch on its hind quarters, making them appear dented. I pinned my focus on the tiny creature, a fresh wave of panic hitting me. It was only a rat, but at the moment, it was also the only other living thing in this cave with me.

Turning my head to keep it in sight set my body swaying, sharp pain piercing my rib. The agony was welcome, keeping my head clearer than it had been. Not everything was numb.

Killion. I sent the plea out telepathically. For once I had to admit defeat. I needed him to rescue me. *Help.*

There was only emptiness, the panic flaring high and bright when he didn't answer. Wherever this was, it had cut off my communication with him.

Was I underground?

The rat stopped and I reached out with my magic to coax it to me. I couldn't breach its mind, however, and it became interested in cleaning its face.

Death? Surely he could still hear me. My magic was dull and sluggish, but still present. If I could stoke it, emit a pulse, it could act as a beacon so he and Killion could find me.

The rat finished its cleaning and started on its path again, sticking close to the wall as it thoroughly checked the floor for any morsel that might be present.

What crumbs would exist in a place like this? Cobwebs hung from the ceilings, nothing but dry stones under foot and dust floating in the air. No one had been here for years, maybe centuries.

As the animal continued on its way, I shoved magic at it. Rats were intelligent, but I could not find the electrical impulses that drove it. Keeping it in my peripheral vision, I watched as it passed behind a long, concrete box. I strained to command it to return.

Focused on the rodent, it took me a moment to realize the box was a sarcophagus—a concrete coffin. On the lid was the sculpture of a man in robes with his arms folded across his abdomen. He held a cross.

My gaze darted around the large room, although turning my head caused me to swivel. Because of the lack of light, I couldn't see too far into the void, but what I could detect caused an involuntary gasp.

There were at least a dozen more coffins surrounding me, and the pieces of the puzzle clicked into place. Catacombs. I was underground. In a cemetery and surrounded by tombs.

As I swayed above my blood, I felt the dead. From inside their stone containers, the skeletons became aware of me as well.

TWENTY-FOUR

I was up a very treacherous creek without a paddle, a scythe, or anything else. I couldn't even feel my hands or arms, and even if I got out of the cuffs, the rest of me wasn't up for an escape.

I am Chloe Frost, I told myself. *Grim Zero incarnate. I do not need to be rescued.*

Forcing myself to breathe through the fiery twinge in my torso, I sucked in oxygen and encouraged my magic to heal me faster. If I could just overcome the venom, my magic could take care of my bonds and get me out of here.

Grim Zero had abandoned me during the fight, but I wasn't letting her off the hook. *You need me,* I told her without preamble. She certainly had to know what was going on.

And you need me. The response came so swiftly, it took me by surprise. I'd anticipated she would remain silent, whatever lesson she wanted to teach me, but all the better that she was willing to talk.

Fine, I conceded. *You're right. I need you.* It was deja vu when my words to King Huvino surfaced. *We're stronger together. You help me and I'll owe you a favor.*

She laughed, the vibration of it tickling my bones. My magic warmed.

You are nothing, Chloe Frost. I could destroy you with a thought.

Okay then. This was going well. *And destroy your latest vessel as well? Mei would love that.*

A snort of disgust.

Neither of us should give her the satisfaction, I said, hoping I was onto something. *It's her fault, you know, not Death's. She's the one who should have saved you. He never had the power to do it.*

Silence. The connection felt open, so I waited. Maybe I'd confused her, or she didn't believe me.

I'm sorry. Not for my resistance to her, but for the way they'd treated her. Being alone in these catacombs, wondering if I'd ever get out, made me realize how hard all this had to be for her. She was stuck inside me because SMG had put her here. She had no say in the matter and surely felt abandoned. *It's just that your power scares me.*

It scares him, too. Death, she meant. *Scares all of you.*

What was it like to be the one entity that Death feared? *I'll make sure you get to talk to him. Together, we'll make him understand.*

A sigh, long and heavy. *Peace. That's all I want. I'm tired.*

She wasn't the only one. *Let's get out of here and I'll do what I can to find that for you.*

Be still. They're coming.

Sure enough, my ears caught the sound of footsteps. While the strigoi were silent predators, down here they feared no one and nothing. I froze, shutting my eyes and allowing my head to fall forward, my hair obscuring my face. *I can't do this on my own.*

You won't have to.

Relief flooded my chest. Had we come to a truce? It seemed like it, and I was going to be true to my word and make sure she got what she wanted.

But first, I had to get out of here.

I didn't dare tip my head up to view my visitors, so I relied on my senses—which, thank goodness, were still working, despite the poison. The strigoi scent was present, but so was...wolf?

Oh no. Not...

"We brought you a present," Lasarus announced, smacking me upside the head. "Wake up, reaper."

Sable lit a nearby wall torch with a snap of her fingers and the room brightened. I feigned grogginess, blinking slowly and letting my mouth hang open. Pretending not to even care, I sent my gaze over him, Sable—who held my scythe—and then the bloody form of Andy's wolf.

He whimpered and growled, but the usually aggressive sound lacked oomph. His eyes were clouded with pain; his front left paw held up as he hobbled on three legs.

Lasarus shoved him to the ground near my dangling feet and he collapsed in the blood pool. Although it was tinged with poison, I wondered if my healing magic had neutralized it by now. The sting inside me lessened with each breath, my energy reviving thanks to Grim Zero's power taking over. Every beat of my heart sent her potency through me, wiping out Sable's influence.

"Your friend here tried to take the blade from us," the strigoi leader sneered. "Him, a shifter, thinking he could take me on?" He laughed and Sable joined in. "But don't worry, that mind trick you did with Pepper won't work with him. I've nullified his magic."

I reached out anyway, attempting to at least soothe my friend.

Get the strigoi to harm you, Grim Zero said. *You need to bleed on the dog.*

He's a wolf, I corrected.

Same difference.

I doubted Andy would agree.

Not relishing the idea of more pain, I knew she and I were on the same page—my blood could now heal more effectively, but the congealed amount on the floor was still too tainted. It would do more harm than good.

"You're nothing but a bully," I muttered. "Picking on those who are weaker than you are so you look tough."

"Is that right?" He moved closer, showing me his fangs. "Maybe I should pick on you, but I have to say, you're not much of a challenge right now."

This time, I managed to spit in his face.

It wasn't much, thanks to my dry mouth, and the impact lacked true shock value. The act was still imperti-nent enough to irritate him and he punched me in the stomach.

I grunted, the chains taking me for a ride. My rib cried out and the claw marks stung, but I contracted my abdominals and as I swung back toward him, drew up my knees and kicked.

The strigoi was too quick, easily dancing out of the way. "Still got a bit of fire in you, I see," he taunted. "Let's see if we can snuff it out."

Sable held up the scythe and twisted it back and forth, the gleam of the torch reflecting on the blade. "I bet I know one way to crush her spirit."

"Don't you dare," I said between clenched teeth. I would not watch another of my friends die at the hand of my weapon. "I'll carve you up if you so much as split a hair on his head."

We need you to bleed, Grim Zero ordered.

I know, I know. I glared at Sable. "Use the weapon on me, not the wolf. Whatever you do to me will affect Killion, remember?"

She cocked her head, smelling a trap. Poor Killion. I hadn't thought about how much pain he had to be in, experiencing all of this along with me.

Sable grinned. "I haven't forgotten anything. Besides, I like to play with wolves."

Kill, the death blade sang.

She moved so fast, I didn't see it coming, the razor-sharp edge slicing through the remnants of my shirt. The cloth fell to the ground next to Andy and fresh blood from the gash running from my collarbone to my navel dripped onto his fur.

Tell him to drink it, Grim Zero ordered.

How without giving away our plan? "You probably shouldn't have done that," I told Sable. "He loves my blood, don't you, Andy?"

I hoped that might nudge the wolf to drink. He didn't, glancing up at me with baleful eyes.

I prodded him with my foot. *Drink, idiot!* "Don't you, Andy? You love the taste of my blood, like all supernaturals. Grim blood."

With the power to heal.

Lasarus registered my scheme right before comprehension lit Andy's vacant stare. The strigoi grasped the wolf by his scruff and tossed him across the room. Andy smacked into the monk's coffin and yelped.

"You are full of deceit," the strigoi snarled at me. Out of the corner of my eye, I saw Andy licking his bloody fur, eyeing us. "I hope Killion dies a hundred times over, just like you will at my hands."

He bit me—another move I wasn't prepared for. His fangs sunk deep into my neck, causing me to cry out. One of his hands held my head in place as he ripped through tendons and sent my body convulsing.

That's when Grim Zero took over, mentally shoving me aside like she'd done previously. This time, I didn't fight it. I let her.

Kill, I encouraged, mimicking the scythe.

I'd seen a few scary creatures in my time as a grim. Never had I been one. Unique, yes. Terrifying? I actually tried not to be. I didn't want folks to fear death or me. I attempted to make dying as painless as possible.

And although I couldn't see the monster I'd turned into thanks to my counterpart, I felt it.

The roar that issued from my mouth would have made a lion shudder. My legs encased Sable's waist like a vise. She jerked backward, her strength and my hold snapping the chains from the secured bolt in the ceiling. No longer without feeling, my hands were a whirlwind of movement, wrapping the length of metal links around her neck.

Lasarus jumped me from behind, taking all three of us to the ground. The impact broke my hold on Sable, but I used the momentum to roll the two of us off her. He ended up under me, her gasping and pulling at the chains now deeply embedded in her windpipe. His hands went around my throat and he squeezed. I punched him in his groin.

Even strigoi have vulnerabilities.

Recovery for them is faster than humans, though, and after his initial shock, he moved to his hands and knees. Meanwhile, Sable gained her feet and snatched a handful of my hair, yanking it. I swiped my fingers through the air and raked her face with them.

Blood was everywhere and I was slick with it—mine and theirs. Lasarus had gotten enough of it from the bite to benefit from its magic. He bounded up, a fighter ready to go.

Revived, Andy leaped into the mix and the four of us became a snarling mess of beasts. I reached for the scythe and Sable beat me to it, raking the weapon across my forearm before she twirled like a dancer and morphed into that hideous creature with the poisonous claws.

I jumped away from the swipe of her hand, which she followed up with the swing of my blade. Nimble as a cat, I steered clear of nails and steel and grabbed her wrist in mid-swipe. I snapped it with barely a thought and she howled in pain, going down to her knees and dropping the scythe.

Andy cried out, too. Lasarus had the upper hand in their fight, pinning the wolf's massive neck under his booted foot. The animal pawed at the air, trying to knock him off, but the strigoi only grinned. "Give me the scythe, or I end him."

Grim Zero didn't hesitate. Not to hand it over and save my friend's life. No, she hurled it at Lasarus' head.

He ducked, forcing him off balance. She—we—pounced.

The vampire and I smacked into the closest coffin, a tangle of teeth and talons. I gave everything I had, but the strigoi now had our blood inside him, making him faster and stronger than he already was.

Commotion broke out behind us, Andy and Sable now going at each other. The blade had disappeared, but I couldn't focus on that right now, everything I had going into the fight with Lasarus and Grim Zero.

He bit me again and I sensed her falter. It was so brief before her next attack, I was unsure I'd actually felt it. But then my body wobbled slightly when he punched my abdomen three times in rapid succession and I found it hard to breathe, the rib firing up again.

We tumbled to the ground, my head smacking the corner of the raised concrete sarcophagus. Inside it, I felt the bones vibrate.

The strigoi used the moment to lift my skull and slam it down again. I saw stars. Grim Zero shook with pain deep within me.

And then I heard her purr through my lips, *"Rise."*

The bones rattled. The ground trembled. The souls of the deceased wailed in my head, my hands automatically covering my ears as if that would help muffle them.

Lasarus didn't notice. He continued to pound my body with his fists, laughing. Andy howled, the sarcophagus split, Sable screamed.

Bits and pieces from the ceiling fell on us as dozens of dead monks came to life, the catacombs trembling. The stone coffins busted to pieces as flesh and bone revived on one skeleton after another.

Lasarus stopped swinging, jumping from me and squawking in shock. A huge chunk of ceiling hit Sable in the head, taking her down. From the splat her skull made, she wouldn't be getting back up.

Andy ran to me, and dizzily, I used his coat to hang onto as I came to my knees, then my feet. Grim Zero smiled, her dead children back from the grave and awaiting her instructions. Lasarus, eyes wide, scanned the sentries now filling the tunnel and pressing in. The ground stopped its shaking, an eerie silence descending on us.

He held out his hands in front of him. "I didn't mean to..."

"Yes, you did," Grim Zero said through my lips. I felt her pull me forward once more. *You've got this.*

I held out my hand and Kill flew into my palm. "You've been reaped."

I swung.

The blade sliced through his neck, sending his head rolling among the debris of the underground burial mound.

As I stared, needing to be sure he didn't resurrect, I felt the weight of dozens of reanimated corpses watching me. Waiting.

Oh boy. *Now what?* I asked my counterpart.

She laughed. *Wait until Death sees this.*

"Chloe!"

"Right on cue," I groaned, holding my side as he appeared in the arched doorway. Killion was beside him, his face ashen.

My soulmate shoved the expressionless zombie monks aside and swept me into a hug. Words in Romanian spilled from his mouth; I understood none of them, but did comprehend their meaning.

"You missed the excitement." I offered what I hoped was a reassuring smile when he set me down and looked me over. His horrified countenance told me just how bad I appeared. "I'm okay, really."

He cut his wrist on my blade's edge and offered it to me as Andy shifted into human form and Death surveyed the damage, including the monks. "Well, this is a pickle, isn't it?"

I sucked in the blood, instantly feeling it aid in my healing. The master vampire held me until I finished a moment later.

Ghost appeared and I let out a joyful holler as I threw my arms around her massive psychopomp neck. "You're okay! Oh my god, don't scare me like that."

She licked my face and I didn't even mind the slobbery mess or the awful dog breath.

"What happened here?" Killion asked through gritted teeth. "Why didn't you wait for me?"

"They ambushed me." The creepy monks continued to simply stare, as if awaiting orders. I shuddered. "Wherever this is."

"We're under the hill," Death said.

I'd suspected as much. "Can you imagine, in our Louisiana soil, trying to carve out tunnels like these?"

"There was no mention of catacombs in the histories," he told me, "but now we know where the lost monks went."

The scent of my blood hung heavy in the air and I felt a bit woozy. Somewhere in the back of my mind, I remembered a mention of them. "The ones who went missing?"

Killion took off his jacket and draped it over my shoulders. "When the brothers took over the hill and insisted God would break the curse, there were many who came and never appeared to leave. The head of the monastery claimed they moved on to other locations, but legend held they simply disappeared."

I glanced at Death. "Didn't you realize they were dead?"

He shrugged. "They weren't on my list, and none of their spirits stayed earthbound."

"So they slipped through the cracks." I glanced at them. "Grim Zero and I raised them; we'll lay them to rest."

"You've had enough for one day," Killion announced.

I was tired, but also renewed. My relationship with her had proven instrumental. "Not even close," I told both of them. "I'm just getting started."

"You don't have to handle this." Death pointed at the monks. "I'll take care of them."

"They're actually the least of my worries."

Killion stiffened. "Then what?"

My skin was sticky with blood. "First, I need to clean up. Then we're going on a hunt."

"I'm in," Andy said, raising a hand. He turned to Death. "And I want Mei off my back. I helped recover the scythe and eliminate the strigoi. It nearly killed me, but I fulfilled my bargain. I don't want her finding another assignment for me. She's as cold-blooded as they come."

"He's right." I gave Ghost a silent command. She stepped toward the closest monk and I touched him with Kill. His spirit left the resurrected body, Ghost latching onto it and disappearing. His bones instantly turned to dust, forming a pile at Death's feet. "Andy's done enough. Any debt still on his back becomes mine."

"I didn't mean—" he stammered, but I cut him off as Ghost reappeared.

"Your debt to SMG is paid." I touched the next monk and Ghost carted his spirit off. "I'll work things out with Mei."

Death said nothing, but assisted me by rounding up the rest of the ghosts so I could return them to their rightful place on the other side of the veil.

When that was done, Killion bundled me up and took me home.

TWENTY-FIVE

Hunting supernaturals of any type is challenging. I suspected hunting a Fae prince and princess even more so.

That's why I called in all of my resources—Aurora, Andy, Killion's vampires, and even Pepper and her sister.

Before we started, Killion insisted on taking me to his penthouse and putting me in the shower. Gently, he washed blood and dust from my hair, massaged the tension from my neck, and cleaned my wounds. He fed me some of his blood, which added to my own healing abilities.

The torn tendons on the top of my shoulder stitched themselves up in record time, as did the cut from my scythe. The deeper gashes made from Sable's nails had closed, but were still pink and puckered. Killion held his hand over them and soon, they were the thinnest of scars. Neither of us was sure if they would ever fully disappear, but even my bruised rib was back to normal in no time.

My mate wasn't. His natural instincts, combined

with our soul bond, made him extra surly because of what had happened. "I should have been there," he groused for the hundredth time, as he helped me tug on my favorite Harry Potter t-shirt. The famous quote from the stories, "I solemnly swear I am up to no good," was scrawled across it in the HP font.

Since becoming a grim, I'd been eating so much and working out, that the added muscle mass and curves made the fabric stretch across my breasts and the sleeves were tight over my new biceps. In only that and my underwear, I noticed the master vampire lick his lips. Soon the shirt was gone and the panties, too.

Making love to him soothed me, and I felt the taut threads of his instincts unwind a bit, too. I was alive and here, in the flesh, and we were together. There was nothing better.

At first, his overprotectiveness had driven me crazy, but he'd explained how the mated bonding had created such fierce need in him to keep me safe and by his side that no amount of logic or objectivity could overcome it. Yes, he knew I was strong and capable. Yes, he understood my need for independence and self-sufficiency. But he couldn't—and wouldn't—stop his desire to be my knight in shining armor and protect me from any and every threat.

An impossible role with me being a grim.

That need was rooted inside me toward him as well, yet I never worried about him. While he was half-human, his vampire side was an elite warrior. He was faster, stronger, and smarter than other supernaturals, and the most intelligent being I'd ever met.

He still saw me as human, albeit one on steroids, with vulnerabilities and weaknesses. I *did* have them, so he wasn't wrong to be concerned about my mortality.

I seemed to have embraced Grim Zero's ability to resurrect myself when needed, but not even Death or SMG could tell me if there was a limit to how many times I could do so in this lifetime. Reapers had certain enhanced abilities in general; being the original grim, I had even more. Neither of us was invincible, though.

Once I was dressed and feeling much more ready to take on the world, I ate three servings of vegetarian lasagna.

Pennyworth corrected Killion—an extremely rare occurrence, "Even if you'd been a bat and flown directly to DuMort Hill, you wouldn't have been there in time to stop Lasarus."

He sipped his wine, still brooding with worry over me, and ignored the well-meaning butler. "Death shouldn't have left you alone."

"He didn't know the strigoi would be there waiting." And I knew my boss was beating himself up over it since he'd patted my back and told me, "Good job. Get some rest," before disappearing when we'd finished. From him, that was a huge compliment, and he didn't give those out *ever*.

Killion's anger rose, his usually hidden fangs making an appearance. "He should have," he snarled.

I shoved away my empty plate and unbuttoned the top of my pants. Good thing my metabolism ran high now, due to the grim energy; I'd be a blimp otherwise. I left the chair and sat in his lap, using my thumb to ease the crease between his brows. "Would you love me if I was fat?"

My touch and the change in subject instantly diffused his anger. He put his arms around my waist. "Your size and shape make no difference to me. You know that."

I did, but I liked hearing it.

Ghost was in her bed by the fireplace and she came to her feet, stretched, and shook herself out, sending hair flying in all directions. It was time to get back to work.

Death had sent her to the clinic when he and I visited the Fae King, so at least she'd been safe. If Lasarus and Sable had gotten to her... I shivered.

Killion read my mind as I hugged the dog and kissed her head. "Do you believe Lasarus kidnapped the princess?"

"I'm inclined to. Where the strigoi stashed her, I have no idea. Oz isn't the most trustworthy being, but he seemed honestly concerned for her, and that's why he sold me out. He probably didn't realize Lasarus was actually after you and had decided I was the best way to get to you."

"Why me?" Killion seemed truly perplexed—another rare occurrence. "Lasarus was one of the most powerful of vampires. What I possess pales in comparison to the wealth and magic he had at his command."

"He didn't have Grim Zero."

"True, but after what you relayed about his intentions toward me, I'm not sure what his end game was. He tried to obliterate both of us, rather than simply snatching you away and hiding you from the world—he could have gone anywhere, you know—he stayed here and used you as bait."

"He claimed he was a collector. He liked unusual magical artifacts, and I happen to be one." I stroked Ghost's fur. "If that's the case, you're right—it would have made more sense for him to kidnap me, as well as Harmony, and suck up our magics." I shrugged. "Maybe he was simply jealous of you."

"Hmm." He finished his wine. "You and Andy search for Harmony. I'll track down her cousin. He and I have things to discuss."

Which, in vampire terms, meant Killion was going to "discuss" Oz right into his grave. "No killing the Fae prince. I have an idea and, if it works, we'll get both of them."

"You have a strategy for this idea?"

"Don't I always?"

My cheeky grin provoked a twitch of his mouth. From him, that was the equivalent of a smile. "I'm not going to like this plan, am I?"

He was going to hate it. I patted his cheek. "It's going to be loads of fun, I promise."

Seeing through the lie, he narrowed his eyes at me. He wanted to make me squirm. "I should lock you up here where you will be safe."

"Katarina has been teaching me escape techniques. Might be cool to see if I've learned anything."

"You are incorrigible."

"Yes," I agreed, taking his hand and drawing him to the bedroom once more. Not for more entertainment, but for a wardrobe change. "And also, I'm eager to have a *discussion* with Prince Oz myself. I just don't want him to realize I'm still alive, and I need Katarina to teach me a new trick."

"Such as?"

"How to look like a vampire."

He seemed put out as we halted at the walk-in closet. "Am I not able to instruct you on such things?"

"My new vibe needs to lean more toward scary Goth girl than come-hither vampire queen."

He chuckled, taking out his cell and dialing her. When she answered, he put her on speaker and I requested her advice. She practically squealed with delight and insisted she had the perfect wardrobe for me —she would bring it over.

While we waited for her to arrive, I told Killion about the alliance I was developing with Grim Zero.

"She's not our enemy," I told him. "But she's tired of the fight, and I think she's lonely."

"What is your solution?"

"She needs time with Death. He's one of the only entities who truly knows her. Who understands her."

He bristled. "That means..."

"I need to spend time with him so she can. It's the only way. I want her to feel appreciated, heard, and respected." I wanted to give her hope. The two of us didn't have long before my contract was up. She deserved to have her say. "I want you present at all times."

His relief was visible. "In case she tries to take over, I should be there."

That *was* a possibility, and he could help shut her

down, but that wasn't the reason. "I want you with me because you're my partner."

This pleased him, and took the edge off his previous anger and feelings of helplessness. "What is this plan to find Harmony?"

We heard Pennyworth answer the penthouse door, and a moment later, Katarina sashayed in, arms full. "Ready?"

"Now or never," I answered, dragging in a fortifying breath. To Killion, I said, "I'll tell you as soon as we're done."

DARKNESS EDGED around us as we gathered in the bar's parking lot. Death snapped a finger and cut out the single light overhead, plunging us deep into the shadows.

"Our main goal is to rescue Harmony," I told the group. Thanks to Katarina, I was dressed in leather from head to toe. My knee high boots had thick soles that gobbled up the pea gravel, crunching under my feet as I paced. My hair was now as a dark as hers, false lashes and heavy makeup made me nearly her twin. She'd even forced me to wear a studded choker around my throat.

A wave of desire rolled over me, coming from Killion. His focused stare sent a shiver up my spine, and I winked at him, promising alone time later. "I want Prince Oz, too," I continued. "If we locate his cousin, I believe we'll have an easy time drawing him to us.

"Killion and Andy, you'll start the search here. See if you can pick up either of their scents, or perhaps Lasarus'. We'll track where they lead."

I'd already explained that the strigoi were all dead and that I wanted the supernatural world to believe I was as well.

"And us?" Katarina waved a ringed finger at the Undead and female shifters near her.

"Find that tour bus they rolled in on the other night. Take it apart, end to end, and make sure there are no hidden compartments where they may have stuffed our girl."

She nodded and motioned at the others. "We're on it. Something that big is hard to hide."

My thoughts exactly. As they disappeared into the shadows, I turned to Aurora and Ghost. "I need you to search the catacombs."

"I thought you and Grim Zero destroyed them." The witch was dressed in black, except for a deep cranberry cape that I coveted. She even had a dramatic heart pin on the collar, an ode to Valentine's Day.

Crud, I'd forgotten about shopping with Nita and what to get Killion. I hadn't seen my phone since Death had spirited me from the clinic. Nita was probably going crazy trying to find me.

No time to worry about that now. "Partially." I should have checked the tunnels thoroughly before letting Killion drag me away, but I'd been ready to leave after all that had occurred. "There is a lot more under that hill—all good hiding places. We need to be sure we check them."

She looked unhappy about it, but picked up the dog and headed for her car. "Be careful, okay?"

"What are we doing?" Death tipped a finger between his chest and mine.

"We're paying King Huvino a quick visit." A chorus of arguments went up from him and Killion, and I silenced them. "We aren't staying, just dropping off an invitation." I glanced at the master vampire. "I'll be back before you know it."

"Do not let her out of your sight," he snarled at Death.

My boss rolled his eyes. "Have you learned nothing? She and Grim Zero took out two strigoi—"

"Three," I corrected. "Using Pepper as a weapon."

Both males glared at me. "Three," Death amended with a huff, "and managed to discover a catacomb filled with lost monks. Without either of us. Trust me, Chloe can handle the Fae king."

"Thank you," I said, a bit cocky.

He grabbed me by the shoulder and we were instantly transported to that realm. It was night there, as well, stars twinkling brightly in the sky. The rolling hills and open fields of wildflowers seemed as alive as they had during the day.

They also became quite aware of us, turning their petaled faces our way.

"You didn't tell me Huvino was a collector of magical artifacts." I made air quotes as we walked. "That's why you assumed my scythe was here."

"It *is* a rare item, but that wasn't my assumption. Like I said, I sensed it was at DuMort Hill, yet not. I thought it was in an alternate dimension."

"The catacombs were like that. I felt it when I was

there. It reminded me of St. Anne's." I shivered at the thought I'd almost been stuck there along with the dead monks.

Sensing my fear of such an event, his carnal power radiated out, protective. "An in-between space. Glad to have Kill back?"

"So glad." The rightness of the compact blade strapped to my back made me smile. "You're coming for dinner tomorrow night. Seven sharp. Killion likes to dress for the occasion, so semi-casual. Don't be late. If you have any dietary restrictions, let Pennyworth know."

He stopped. "What?"

I passed him. "You heard me." Raising my voice, I called, "King Huvino? It's me, Chloe. Sorry to barge in again, but I wanted to extend an invitation—"

Two of his guards instantly appeared. They pointed their long spears at us and told us to march. Death started to argue, but I grabbed his sleeve. "Just go with it."

We weren't brought into any type of grand castle. Instead, the king was bathing, sans clothes, in a moonlit pool. I tried not to stare when he rose from the water, dripping, and accepted a robe from one of his minions. He was exceptionally buff for an old guy. "How is it you keep disturbing my peace?"

"It's not like I can text you and ask for admission to your realm." I glanced at him once he was covered. "*Is* there a way for me to contact you without dropping in unannounced?"

"Think carefully before you respond," Death said.

The king chuckled. "You suspect she'll abuse my generosity?"

"She does mine."

I smacked Death's arm. Which was dumb, since it was hard as the nearby boulder and I had to shake out my fingers from the pain that bloomed in them.

The king leaned against said boulder, watching us. "Ignore him," I told Huvino. "If you have a preferred way for me to speak to you in the future, I promise not to bother you unless it's an emergency."

"What is this invitation, Grim?"

Okay, so he wasn't going to share. Fine. Maybe after I resolved the Oz and Harmony mystery, he'd feel differently about me.

"Can you sense Harmony with your blood connection to her? Most supernaturals who share such a bond can in our realm."

"If I'm close enough, yes. Since I'm here and she isn't, I can't locate her."

"But you could if you came with us, right?"

"What are you suggesting?"

I grinned and Huvino and Death gawked when I explained what I wanted the king to do.

TWENTY-SIX

"Harmony isn't here presently," Killion reported when Death and I returned to the bar's parking lot with Huvino in tow. He raised a brow at me and I introduced them quickly before he continued. "Nor has she been tonight."

Huvino sniffed the air and made a face at the greasy, stale beer odor that hung like fog around the place. "Why would she come to a location such as this?"

I'd taken a page from Katarina's playbook and dressed Harmony's father like an aging punk rock star. His hair was spiked, he wore black eyeliner, and like me, sported way too much leather. "A lot of supernaturals hang out here."

I decided to save the details of why and how they often entertained themselves by preying on unsuspecting mortals.

"Her entourage is inside," Killion told us, "including the prince."

"Oz is here?" The king started for the door, muttering

nasty names under his breath. "I will throttle him and remove his—"

I stopped him. "Remember the plan? He thinks I'm dead and won't be expecting either of us. Our first priority is to find your daughter, then we'll deal with Oz."

He didn't appreciate being touched and his face twisted with disgust as he pointedly removed my hand from his arm. "If she's not here, where is she?"

"I was hoping you could help locate her."

"Andy is following her scent," Killion told us. "I stayed here to keep tabs on the prince."

And probably hoping to catch him and have that 'discussion' he yearned for.

Huvino closed his eyes for a brief moment, his eyeballs moving under his lids. Then he opened them. "It's faint, but I'd say she's south."

Aurora and Ghost came chugging in and she parked in one of the last vacant slots. "No sign of her," she announced, getting out. Ghost greeted me and surveyed the group with a wagging tail. "We scanned the whole place and the only living things inside it were a few rats. How they survive there is beyond me."

I made introductions again and then told her, "They're ghosts." It had dawned on me after I'd seen the same one in Killion's bathroom, skittering along the baseboards after my shower. There were absolutely no vermin in his hotel, and I knew it was the exact same guy, the odd dent in his back end a sure giveaway. He'd no doubt followed us there, ghosts able to travel easily across spaces. I'd kept this detail to myself and quietly touched it with the scythe when Killion was occupied, sending it to the afterlife.

Sometimes the dead were so real to those of us who could see and hear them, we assumed they existed in the land of the living. "Ah." She nodded. "That must be it."

"Andy is probably in wolf form," I told her, relating what Killion had said about him tracking Harmony. "Is there any way you can communicate with him and see if he's picked up on her travels after she left here the other night?"

Her eyes flashed the sapphire blue of her panther and her face took on a faraway look. I assumed she was telepathically connecting to him. "He's outside your apartment."

I shared a frown with Killion and Death. I hadn't yet officially moved in with the master vampire, but I spent less and less time at my place. "Why would she have gone there?"

"Perhaps she wished to be friends with you," King Huvino offered, a hopeful note in his voice.

Not likely, but all parents wanted to believe the best of their kids, didn't they?

"Her scent is strong," Aurora continued, those beautiful, yet eerie eyes staring off into the darkness on the edge of the parking lot. "Andy is drunk on it."

"She's there *now*?" My stomach felt queasy. If she'd harmed my landlady, I'd skin her alive. "Is Vera home?"

A pause as Aurora refocused. My pulse pounded. My legs wanted to move, to run to her, make sure she was safe. "She's downstairs watching Wheel of Fortune."

My breath whooshed out. "You're sure she's okay?"

"He saw her pass the window carrying a cat."

Again, I felt a wave of relief. "Tell him I'm on my way and to be careful."

"You believe she's there?" Huvino asked.

The two-story was seven or eight miles away. I wasn't sure how close he had to be for his blood detector to work. "Focus again. Can you feel her?"

He shook his head. "I sense Oz and the females with him most strongly, but Harmony is...muted."

"Can the prince sense you?" Killion asked, suddenly tense.

As if in answer, the male in question stepped out the front door, stopping under the flashing beer signs to look at our group. I pivoted Huvino toward the shadows, myself as well. "Our cover may be broken."

"Y'think?" Death half sat on the hood of a car, arms crossed, his tone full of impertinence. "Brilliant, Chloe."

Killion snarled at him.

Death grinned.

I grabbed Aurora's arm, snapping her out of her trance, and propelled her toward the prince, standing on the rotten wood landing and scrutinizing us.

At least he hadn't recognized me or Huvino.

Yet.

"Intercept him," I told her *sotto voce*. "Use your charms on him and get him back inside."

"Hello, handsome," she crooned, swaggering toward the entrance. Power and sexuality oozed off her.

Oz didn't pay her any attention. "You there," he called to me. "Do I know you?"

Killion stepped in front of me and Huvino, shielding

us. "We met the other night." He walked toward the entrance, pointing at Death to send the prince's attention in that direction, while motioning my boss forward. "This is my friend, DuMort. I wanted to introduce you."

I hid a smirk at the name. My boss cut his eyes to me, then followed Killion. "You don't belong here," he said to Oz and I cringed. "Best you return to your own realm."

Great. Death, of course, had decided to override my plan.

I couldn't see the prince's face, but the pregnant pause told me what I needed to know. He recognized Killion and the magic simmering under his skin was about to send him running.

And if he could create portals like the king, we'd never catch him.

With a quiet command in her ear, I set Ghost on the ground, then hastily drew a binding spell in the dirt with one toe. She ran toward Oz and I sent the magic in the same direction with an arrow in the dirt. If he escaped, we might not ever find Harmony. "Can you take us to my place?" I murmured to Death. "All of us. Now?"

The air changed, vibrating, but it wasn't because he was doing as I'd ordered. It was the Fae prince's magic sparking. "Grab him!" I yelled at Ghost and flung a handful of bespelled dirt in his direction.

He raised a hand to tear a hole in the dimensional fabric and escape. Ghost morphed and clamped onto his wrist, and the dirt changed to sparkling magic in the air, raining down on him at the same moment.

He yelped, she growled, and Oz froze as the spell hit.

Aurora gave me a pleased look. "We might make a proper witch out of you yet."

Death gave a lazy eye roll before he waved his hand in a circle.

Instantly, we landed behind my apartment. I slammed into the gate of the fenced backyard, ricocheting off it and into Killion's arms. He righted me, and I glanced around at the assorted heaps of Aurora, Huvino, and Oz—still held by my psychopomp.

As each of them gained their feet, Aurora hurriedly brushing at the dust and grass on her cloak, Huvino seemed impressed.

Andy was on the stair landing that led to my apartment. He instantly morphed from wolf to man, looking entirely blitzed out. "She's so perfect," he said, dreamily.

With a swift dive into her bag, the witch brought out what looked like a bath bomb and tossed it into the air. It instantly exploded and everyone sneezed, including me.

"That should do it," she said, nodding. "I worked up a faster way to anesthetize us from her seductive powers."

The king blustered, but I silenced him with a glance. "We can't function if she's beguiling us, intentionally or not." I faced Death and Killion and made a twirling motion with my finger. "Bubble."

Whenever we were around my nosy landlady, who insisted I never have a man at the apartment, we needed a cone of silence or she would run out of the house to see what we were doing. Both lifted a hand to do as I requested, saw each other and stopped. Surprisingly, my boss motioned for Killion to do the honors. He did, and Killion's magic wrapped around the group.

Oz focused on me and I slid in front of Huvino, hoping to keep the king's presence a secret a little longer. "But you're..." His lips worked, nothing else making it past them as he put two and two together.

"Dead?" I supplied. "Almost, but you failed. Again. How long have you been in cahoots with Lasarus and Sable?"

"Cahoots?" Andy snickered. "You sound like my grandma."

"What*ever*," I gave him a *shut up* glare. "How long have you been in league with the strigoi?"

"Why are we here?" Oz scanned the yard and apartment, pretending he didn't know. "Why are you dressed like that? And why is this thing"—he tried to shake off Ghost's toothy grip—"biting me?"

"I'm asking the questions." And I didn't appreciate him calling my dog a 'thing.' "Why did you set me up?"

"What are you accusing me of?"

Death crossed his arms and glared. "Answer her."

The prince shrugged, then clamped his lips together.

Bad move. Before Killion or Death could use force to make him talk, I intervened with a mental order to them to stand down and let me handle this. "The night at the bar," I said to Oz, "you called the strigoi and alerted them we were there. Your Fae hearing picked up on the fact we planned to apprehend Harmony, so you needed a distraction, didn't you? She was using her scent to beguile humans, and you were handing them over to Lasarus and Sable."

"Why would I do such a thing? They are quite capable of getting their own *snacks*."

Talk about poor word choice—he was really getting on my nerves. "Was it blackmail? They threatened Harmony. At least Lasarus did. A Fae princess next in line to the throne—that's a rare artifact."

He stiffened and I knew I was on the right track. Huvino stepped from behind me. "That vampire was after my daughter? *You*." He drew the word out and shook a finger at the prince. "This is all your fault."

Oz's brows shot to his hairline. "King Huvino?" He blinked, then bowed deeply. "My only wish has been to protect her."

"By offering up Chloe and myself?" Killion's irises went red with anger.

Oz raised a placating hand. "It wasn't like that. Lasarus said he wanted the scythe. He promised to leave Harmony alone if I got it for him."

I stood shoulder to shoulder with the king. "He lied, and now you're lying to cover your backside."

He drew himself up a notch. "I am not."

"How did you bypass the wards at the penthouse and let them in?" Killion stepped to my other side, forming a wall. "Only Death is able to breach them."

My boss grinned. "And I bloody well wouldn't let the strigoi in."

"I used compulsion on the front desk clerk," Oz admitted.

Oki, the vampire who manned the reception area, was now out of a job. I could intervene on her behalf, but she was Killion's employee. The safety of the hotel was paramount for many reasons.

"The night at the arboretum." Aurora stomped

toward the prince. "You killed my mate!" She slapped him so hard, he fell to the ground.

Andy put an arm around her waist, hauling her back before she launched her next attack. "Whoa there, witchy woman. I'm okay."

"How can you not want revenge?" she snapped.

Andy turned her in his arms and smiled down into her face. "So we're mates, are we?"

"Ugh!" She stomped her heel on the top of his foot, and he howled, releasing her and dancing back.

"Shifters," she groused. I couldn't help my chuckle.

"The bomb wasn't my idea." Oz wiped at the blood on his lip. Ghost tugged on his wrist and he rose to his feet. He eyed Aurora warily. "That was all Lasarus."

I glanced at Killion. Usually, he could smell a lie on someone, and I was pretty sure the prince was telling tall tales. "Did you ever know Lasarus to have a thing for blowing up people?"

The master vampire's return look was granite. "Not his style. He preferred being up close and personal when he killed."

Oz picked up on the fact we were speaking of Lasarus in the past tense. "Wait, is he dead?"

Death sighed dramatically. "Is the girl inside or not?"

"How would I know? I do not have to answer these ridiculous questions. You have no jurisdiction over the Fae!"

Ghost drooled on his pant leg and gave his arm a shake. He yelped and demanded I order her to release him.

I didn't. Not because I thought Oz would get away, but because he deserved it.

"Death may not have jurisdiction over you, but I do," the king said, stepping forward. "Answer him. Is Harmony inside this"—he gave the house a brief look of disgust—"abode?"

Oz scanned his outfit, as if noticing it for the first time. "Why are you dressed like that?"

"Oh, for reaper's sake! Enough with this." As planned, I unsheathed my scythe and handed it to the king. "Finish it."

TWENTY-SEVEN

Oz blanched. "*What?*"

Huvino took the weapon, holding it up and eyeing the clean steel with reverence. A slice of moonlight kissed the blade and reflected in his eyes. "Yes, it's time for justice."

Ghost made a quiet noise deep in her throat that sounded like a chuckle.

Oz cursed under his breath, and I saw the wheels turning in his head. He once again searched for an escape. "Call off your mutt," he demanded, wrenching his arm from her teeth.

"*Mutt?*" If I'd had the blade, I would have swung it at him. Since I didn't, I stepped forward and punched him in the face.

Blood sprayed from his nose, and he dropped to the ground like a sack of gravestones. "Don't you ever say that again." I was rather fond of mixed breed "mutts," but coming from him it was an insult.

He spit blood on the ground, a glob hitting the side of

Katarina's boot. She would not be happy. "You've lost your senses," he snarled. "You're a maniac."

I'd been called a lot of things in the past few days, but what I was was an angry Grim Reaper. I so wanted to take it out on him, but I needed answers. The king's daughter was either an innocent in Oz's game, or a participant. Either way, this ended tonight. "Why is Harmony here?" I demanded, kicking the sole of his loafer.

"How would I know?"

Using some dead grass to wipe the grossness off the leather, I wondered if I could borrow Pennyworth's stash of shoe polish. "You don't seem like the brightest bulb in the box." I motioned for Killion and Death to follow me up the steps. "My guess? You put her here after Lasarus didn't hold up his end of the bargain you made with him, hoping to incriminate me in her kidnapping."

The three of us took the steps to my back door. Inside, the girl lay on my bed, looking every bit like Sleeping Beauty waiting for her prince.

The king burst in behind us, made a soft noise, and called her name. She did not stir.

"Drugged?" I asked.

Killion shook his head. "I don't smell anything like that." He cocked his chin at Death. "You?"

Death frowned. "She's in stasis. Like a coma."

"So she *is* Sleeping Beauty," I murmured.

The king sat on the edge of the mattress and cradled her to him. "Harmony, wake!"

"Someone has to kiss her," Aurora declared and cut her gaze to Andy. The two of them stood shoulder to shoulder in the doorway. "Not you."

"I don't understand." The king glanced at me. "No one shall dare to kiss her!"

"It's the way fairytales work in our world." He gave me a look like I was nuts. "Don't worry, we can try something else."

"Yeah," Death said, "like finding out why Oz put her in stasis to begin with. He can bring her out of it, correct?"

"This is not Fae magic." Huvino rocked her back and forth. "My poor Harmony. I should never have let him take you from me."

"She smells familiar," Killion said, moving closer, nose twitching like a cat's. I hoped Aurora had another of those spell bombs to throw in the air, but then he glanced at me. "Much like the odor on you when we found you."

Death snapped his fingers. "You're right."

"Sable's poison?" I couldn't help it, I took a step back. The memory of the pain that venom had caused me made me want to run. "Why hasn't it killed her?"

"Because she's not of this realm." Death held a hand over her, scanning her body. "It doesn't work the same on her as it does on humans."

Indignation colored my voice. "I'm human."

He dropped his hand. "And an annoying one at that."

"Can't you do something?"

"I'm not a healer, you know that."

Aurora fiddled around in her bag. "I can put together a potion."

"I need to take her home," Huvino said. He laid her down and snatched up the scythe. "First, I'm going to remove the prince's manhood and shove it down his—"

Eww. "Whoa, whoa, whoa." The thought of my blade touching anything below the guy's belt made me nauseous. "I'll let you threaten him, but we agreed no chopping off body parts or killing, remember? You can pretend you're going to, but no actual harm can come to him from my blade." In the distance, I heard Ghost growl. On second thought... I grinned. "Although, he might make a better tree than a prince."

Huvino mirrored my smile.

"Chloe," Death warned.

"Stop saying my name that way. It's getting old."

"Stop being impertinent and reckless, and I won't need to."

Killion snarled, territorial. "Speak to her like that again and we'll have words, you and I."

"Uh oh." I clucked my tongue. "When Killion wants to have a 'discussion,' you're in big trouble."

Death glanced at the master vampire before he winked at me. "Pretty sure I can take him."

Talk about impertinent. Killion's already aggravated temper went Code Red, and I stepped between them just before he reached for my boss' neck. "Stop it, both of you. We fix Harmony now and work out our personal issues over dinner tomorrow night."

Killion gave me a what-the-bloody-reaper-are-you-talking-about look. "Dinner?"

Oops. "Did I forget to mention I arranged with Pennyworth for the *four* of us to get together and chat?" I emphasized the number, hoping he would catch on.

He did, but was having none of it. "He is not, and never will be, invited to my home."

Death, who earlier had no desire to attend, now seemed eager. "Come on, Fang Boy." I cringed—Killion only ever let me call him that. "Chloe's trying to do a nice thing. You don't want to let her down now, do you?"

It took Andy, Aurora, and me to wrestle Killion off him after that.

Huvino watched in shock, yet equally fascinated, as we eventually separated them and I dragged Killion outside.

"What the reaper was that?" I asked, panting from the exertion.

His irises were red-ringed, his fangs on full display. "He's disrespected you one too many times. I will not stand for it."

While the ongoing battle between them was always edgy, I suspected this was left over anxiety from my encounter with Lasarus and Sable. Reprimanding him wouldn't help. I needed to distract him until I could get him home and help him burn off that energy. An idea popped into my head. "I want you to take me to Romania. It's on my bucket list."

His brows dipped. "What?"

"You heard me." It was something I'd been thinking about for a while, even before our bonding. Ever since I'd recovered his family ring and then psychically transported to the castle where he'd been born, I wanted to learn more. "I want to see that castle you inherited. Maybe for Christmas. I bet it's pretty then, up in the mountains."

"Can you put your vacation plans on hold for a lousy minute?" Oz called from below. "I demand my freedom!"

"Shut up." Killion waved a hand at him. A human would fall asleep at the magic. Oz didn't, but he did become mute. The vampire pulled me close and lowered his voice to a seductive level. "I know what you're doing and it won't work."

Sure it would. I could already sense his rage morphing into desire. "How about this?" I kissed him, drawing his lips to mine and not letting go until his body relaxed in my arms.

Both of us were breathing heavy when the others emerged, crowding us on the landing. I broke away, unable to hide my smile as Killion cleared his throat and attempted to shut down the overflowing lust magic flying around us.

"It worked," Aurora announced, coughing a little.

"Your potion?"

She shook her head. "A kiss."

Harmony stuck her head out the exit, grinning from pointy ear to pointy ear.

"You kissed her?" I asked the witch under my breath.

"Not me." She waved the princess out and Harmony tugged on someone's waist. "Him."

The wicked smile on Aurora's face told me something was up. As Harmony stepped fully onto the landing, Death emerged in her wake.

He was *not* smiling.

I stepped down one rung, covering my lips with my hand. Laughter still bubbled out, earning me the Death Glare.

"Hey, bestie," Harmony said, eyeing me. "Thanks for hooking me up with this big guy." She waggled her brows and placed a hand on Death's chest. "Talk about a good kisser."

"You?" Killion smirked and Death sent him the scowl that could strike down mere mortals. "That's absolute karma right there."

Death was now the one in Code Red territory. Again, I hid a delighted smile.

"Well, I didn't see you stepping up to do it," he growled at Killion.

Huvino was next to join us, all of us moving down the stairs until we hit the bottom. "We must go," the king announced, wiggling a finger at his daughter. He cocked his chin at me, then at Oz. "I trust you'll take care of that traitor. You are free to handle him as you see fit. He violated the rules of this realm, and should pay the price for it according to your laws."

Harmony walked to the prince and spit on him.

The act warmed my heart. While I had no intention of becoming besties with a Fae princess, we might still be friends.

She grabbed my arm and dragged me away from the others before lowering her voice. "You won't believe what he did to me. I'll tell you all about it at dinner."

"Dinner?"

Huvino took my hand and Killion tensed. "Grim, it appears it is I who owe *you* a favor. My daughter and I have things to work out, but you have given us a second chance at it. Thank you." He kissed the top of my hand. "Until we meet again."

The father and daughter began to walk away, Harmony throwing a seductive look over her shoulder at

Death and offering a wink. Her magic tickled my nose. We might need a lot more of Aurora's bombs.

"King Huvino?" I called.

He glanced back. "Hmm?"

I held out my hand. "The scythe?"

His smile was cunning and not repentant in the least. "Of course." He handed it to me. "It must stay in this realm."

And in my hand.

"See you tomorrow," Harmony called. She waved at Death before disappearing through one of the portals with her father.

I rounded on my boss. "You invited her to dinner?"

He held up both hands as if to fend me off. "She asked what I was doing tomorrow night and I told her. She invited herself."

Killion chuckled. "Death has a girlfriend."

"It's not funny," I chided. "Grim Zero..." I stopped. She'd been surprisingly quiet during all this. Not good. Not good at all. "Un-invite Harmony," I demanded. "She can't come."

Death sighed, then his voice took on the timbre that rattled my bones, booming inside our bubble. "I have absolutely no interest in a Fae princess."

It was said to reassure Grim Zero, not me. "She's not deaf, you know." I sent my awareness inside and sensed her behind the wall. *You okay?*

Grim Zero: *If she touches him again, I will kill her.*

Okay then.

"We good?" Death asked, seeing my face.

"Undecided. Could go either way."

Killion motioned at Oz. "What about him?"

What better way to work off his anxiety over me than by beating up a no-good Fae prince who'd tried to kill us both? "He's all yours."

The master vampire's eyes flashed with a predatory gleam.

"I want in," Death said.

We all gaped at him.

He peered down his nose at us. "No one messes with my favorite grim and gets away with it."

"I'm your favorite?" I grinned and punched his ribs lightly. "I knew it!"

Solidarity between the two males seemed to lock in, a mental exchange going back and forth between them. Usually I could hear Killion's thoughts but I didn't need to. The look on his and Death's faces told me all I needed to know.

Oz yelled and struggled harder, his blood now dripping from Ghost's mouth. "You can't do this! Send me back! I'm a prince!"

"The church?" Killion asked Death.

Death nodded. "That'll do."

Killion kissed my forehead. "I'll see you at home."

In the blink of an eye, they disappeared.

"Not sure I dig this fashion choice," Aurora said, bumping my elbow with hers.

I was cold now that the adrenaline had worn off and the night had grown chilly. "You could loan me that cloak to cover up."

"Not a chance in Hades, but nice try."

"Chloe?" My landlady's shrill voice rang out from the backyard.

Reapers, creepers, when Killion and Death had left, so had the bubble. "Yes, Vera, it's me. Sorry to bother you."

The gate squeaked as she barreled through it, dressed in her night clothes. One side of her hair was smashed against her head, the other fluffy curls. "It's one in the morning and it's freezing out here. Come inside." She narrowed her eyes and took in my clothes, hair, and makeup. "Goodness, Chloe, that's an odd look for you."

Katarina slid from the shadows. I wondered how long she'd been there. "Hey, Miss Vera. I'm Kat. Chloe and I were attending a costume party tonight, dressed as twins. What do you think?"

The elderly woman's eyes widened at the vampire, but she recovered quickly, waving us inside. "How fun. Let's get some hot cocoa and you can tell me all about it."

I sent Katarina a look and she slung an arm around me, grinning.

TWENTY-EIGHT

The next evening at dinner, I was once again dressed in clothes that were not my style. The slinky black velvet gown went to the floor and had a deep V in the back. Matching stilettos cramped my toes, but at least I didn't turn my ankles when I walked. Being bonded to a vampire had its advantages, including enhanced balance.

The lights were low, the candles lit, the fireplace crackling. Ghost slept in her bed near the hearth, and Corvus watched the proceedings with his black, beady eyes. He kept his comments to himself, which was unusual, but I appreciated it. His time with Patty was paying off.

Killion sat at his normal place at the head of the table, dressed in his finest suit, a rich black that matched my attire. He'd gone sans tie, leaving his silk shirt unbuttoned at the neck, subtly mimicking the V of my dress.

Death had shown up exactly at seven, not a second early or late. He cleaned up nicely, sporting a gray suit that shimmered in the candlelight. He'd put product in his hair, combing the currently raven black tresses back and showing off his incredible cheekbones.

Pennyworth outdid himself with the seven-course meal, but I barely tasted the food. Nerves kept my stomach tight, and waiting for my counterpart to speak kept my thoughts spinning.

She was hardly immune to Death's good looks, my whole body warming whenever he engaged me in conversation. The fact that he'd shown up to talk to her pleased her immensely, yet she remained silent. It seemed as if she were simply soaking him in.

A weighted air hung between the three of us, the males seemingly on edge, too. Patiently waiting. We ate, made polite conversation, and Killion more than once arched a brow at me. *Well...?*

I shrugged. *She's not saying anything.*

All I could do was keep encouraging her.

Me: *This is your chance. You wanted to talk to him, so talk.*

GZ: *I am unsure of what to say.*

Me: *You're kidding, right?*

GZ: ...(silence)

Me: *After so many years and all that's happened, it's understandable that you might feel shy about launching into it.*

GZ: *I hate him.*

Not what I was anticipating, but, Me: *Okay. Is that where you want to start?*

GZ: *No, no, no. I love him, too.*

This was going to be all kinds of fun. I glanced up

from my blackened swordfish with brown butter and capers to find the males had stopped discussing the economy and were staring at me. Again. "I need more wine," I said, even though my glass was half-full. "Anyone else?"

I ran to the kitchen with the goblet, stopping just inside the door to lean on the island countertop. Penny-worth looked up, alarmed. "Are you unwell?"

Damn straight. "I'm... Unsure." It was the best word to describe it. "Maybe this was a bad idea."

Laughing came from the dining room. Pennyworth went to the freezer and withdrew a carton of my favorite ice cream. He handed it to me along with a spoon. "Sounds like the master and Death have bonded. How can that be a bad thing?"

They had indeed, although *bonded* might have been a strong word and this new connection seemed to be over the justice they'd doled out to Oz, rather than dinner. I popped a spoonful of the soothing dessert into my mouth, let it melt. "This is supposed to be for Grim Zero but she is on an emotional rollercoaster right now and I don't know how to make it work. I thought this would be easier."

"When I have uncomfortable things to discuss with Omwee, I can be the same way. All I wish to do is climb into bed with a fat slice of chocolate cake and stream meaningless TV."

Sounded good to me. "And do you?"

"I've learned there is a time to talk and a time not to. When the time is right, we must speak from our heart and save the food coma for those other times."

I sucked down another helping of creamy goodness. "I struggle just to find the words I need to express myself. Speaking for someone else is definitely a challenge."

He took the carton from me. "It remains heartfelt. You have two dominate males in the other room who want the best for you. You *are* Grim Zero. The only one here tonight who should be nervous is Death."

We were having fondue for dessert and he handed me skewers and a plate of freshly cut fruit for dipping. He gathered the rest.

"I *am* Grim Zero," I muttered. Maybe if I said it enough times, I would truly believe it. There were definitely times when I had embraced her and that magic, but more often than not I'd felt she was separate from me.

Everything we'd shared, every enemy we'd faced, the times her necromancy—*my* necromancy—had saved my life, I owed her. How could she have done all that if we were truly separate?

"Holy cow," I said, sagging against the island.

"What?" Pennyworth asked.

I'm sorry, I told her. *Maybe it's me, not Death, you should take to task.*

She didn't agree nor disagree. In fact, it felt more like she sighed. Relaxed.

She was lonely because I'd shut her out. Sad and angry because I hadn't accepted her fully. All those times she'd helped me, it was because she'd wanted to, not because she had to.

Was it possible she *liked* me?

My chest warmed and my nerves vanished. "I am

Grim Zero," I said again, and this time it felt normal. Right.

Pennyworth smiled and it lit up his face. "She's okay, now?"

My entire being felt filled with quiet acceptance. Peace.

There were still things that needed to be said. "Thank you." I kissed the butler's cheek. "I'll save that cake and binge TV for another time."

"Topped with ice cream?"

"You know it."

Together, we hauled the fondue items to the table. I took my seat, looked at Death, and spoke my mind.

TWENTY-NINE

Valentine's Day arrived with me at the clinic for my shift. Harlow had informed me that while she liked animals, she never wanted to fill in for me again. I offered apologies and sent her a gift box of her favorite candies.

I held onto my guilt over Cron and Mags' deaths. At least Oki had evaded Killion's wrath. He'd stewed about it, but ultimately concluded his security system was flawed, not the vampire. Offering Aurora a healthy sum, he'd requested she add an additional layer of security to the hotel. She'd placed spells on obsidian stones to create immunity to compulsion from any supernatural, and all staff members were required to carry one while working.

In order to reassure Omwee, and add yet another protection to the penthouse, Killion had assigned the reclusive vampire a new job—to stand guard outside our private quarters when the master vampire and I were not in attendance. Pennyworth would not be caught by surprise ever again, and Omwee had seemed relieved by the arrangement.

That evening, Killion and I met Nita and JR for dinner at the new restaurant in town. My best friend had been upset about me ghosting her, but forgave me when I explained about the phone. Killion had provided me with an upgraded replacement, and I took the first picture on it of the four of us in front of the restaurant's wishing well. Vampires could be caught on digital cameras, and although Killion resisted ever having his likeness taken, he was a good sport about it.

The food was delicious, but not as much as Pennyworth's. I knew he would secretly be pleased when I told him. We had a lovely time, and the sparks between my two friends were evident. *I knew it*, I said to Killion as Nita laughed at a story JR told about the hamster who'd bitten him earlier at the clinic. She made over his bandaged thumb and stroked the scar over his brow that I had given him long ago when we were kids.

From the other side of the room, Mason gave me a covert wave. Across the table from him, Megan blushed. They were enjoying their own dinner. He was in a suit that made him look like a mini-Killion, and she wore her usual black everything.

Killion caught my glance at them and squeezed my knee under the table. He'd convinced me to wear the sexy black dress and heels again. *Your matchmaking is second to none.*

While I couldn't technically take credit for Mason and Megan, I'd been trying to set up JR and Nita since he'd moved back to town. I asked about his mom and he assured me she was doing well after beginning a regiment of Aurora's teas. "They smell and taste awful," he said, making a face, "but they're magic. She has so much energy and all her tests show she's in remission."

Little did he know just how much "magic" they were. Aurora should market them. "I'm so happy for her, and you. I sense she'll recover in no time."

"She asked me to invite the two of you to brunch next Sunday if you're available." He squeezed Nita's hand. "She insists I need more friends."

All eyes swung to Killion. Even when he wasn't trying to, he exuded authority and command. His word was golden. A smile graced his lips and he glanced at me, silently asking if I wanted to. I did. He dipped his chin. "We'd be honored."

JR, as well as Nita, beamed, and we ordered dessert.

Later, when we'd eaten our fill and were leaving, Killion handed me a gold coin. "Make a wish."

Closing my eyes for a heartbeat, I saw my desire in my mind and tossed the coin into the water.

He steered me out the door to the waiting limo and we climbed inside with my friends. The February night was unusually warm and he utilized the roof window, allowing the silvery moonlight to slide over us as we drove through town. We dropped the two of them at Nita's to pick up her car before they headed to Darcy's party. Thankfully, I'd gotten out of that one.

Once we said our goodbyes and were on our way, he asked, "What did you wish for?"

"I can't tell you or it won't come true."

He drew me close and nuzzled my ear. "We don't have to wait until Christmas to travel to the castle."

"You," I sighed. It hadn't been hard for him to guess. I bared my neck to his lips. "It will give me something to look forward to. I finish my degree in December and I'll need a break. In the meantime, you can teach me Romanian."

His mouth trailed across my jaw. "What would you like to learn first?"

"Duh. Food."

A chuckle. His lips caught my ear lobe. "How about anatomy? *Lobul urechii*." A finger trailed over my neck. "*Gât*." It touched my bottom lip. "*Buze*."

Shivers raced over my skin. It wasn't the words themselves, but the way he said them. "I didn't realize learning a new language could be so sexy." I kissed him, long and slow, and then pulled back. "I'm sorry."

"For what?"

"I didn't get you anything for Valentine's Day. You were so generous to invite my friends for dinner and pick up the tab. And the only language I can teach you is veterinary terms. Like *debridement* and *hebephrenic nerve*. Super sexy, I know."

"Your happiness is the only thing I desire. And you're wrong—you did give me a gift."

"I did?" Had Nita or Pennyworth gotten something for him and slapped my name on it? I tried to look in the know. "Oh, right, of course. That...uh...thing."

He smiled, drawing me into his lap. My dress rose high on my thighs and he gently caressed them. "You allowed me to exact revenge on the prince after he participated in the plan to end us."

I made a face. "That's not a present."

"To me, it is." He touched my streak of now-violet colored hair. "You are soft-hearted and I love that about you, but he needed to be dealt with. He was also an example of what will happen to anyone who tries to harm you. You are my bonded mate. No one will assume they can hurt you and not suffer for it."

While Killion and Death had done a number on Oz, they both knew his death would weigh heavy on me and therefore spared his life.

They'd forced him into his worst nightmare instead, returning him to the land of the Fae and King Huvino. While the leader had left justice up to us, it seemed my two benefactors felt the king would enjoy closure over what Oz had done. Last we'd heard, Oz was waiting on the king and tending to his massive gardens, all while being denied the use of magic. He'd become a mundane overnight and the manual labor was killing him.

"Not high on the romance quotient." I tugged on a lock of hair that had fallen across Killion's forehead. "But if you're happy, I'm happy."

He removed a square wooden box from his inner pocket. "How does this rate on the romance scale?"

My heart thudded hard against my ribs. Words caught in my throat, the sudden constriction making it too tight to breathe.

"This is not a traditional proposal." He rubbed a thumb over the inlaid wood. The carvings on the top and sides were intricate. "Yet, it is a very old family custom."

What did that mean? "Pro...pos..." I couldn't get the word out.

He placed the box in my palm and magic zinged up my arm. Along with the symbols, there was a design that I recognized from the lost family ring I'd retrieved for him. "Killion...I..." My voice shook. Coherent thought escaped me.

His smiled deepened as he felt my struggle. Wrapping one of his much larger hands around mine, he steadied my shaking fingers. "I'm rushing you, but we don't have long to be together in this lifetime."

My contract, over in a few short years. His bond to me, which would cause him to die when I did. How had I gotten so lucky to find him? "Please, keep rushing me," I whispered, as tears filled my eyes.

His chuckle was lighthearted and he caressed my cheek before he opened the box. "This was my mother's."

The ruby glinted in the moonlight, sucking away what little breath I had recovered. "It's a twin to yours."

"Passed down on my father's side," he explained, "and he gave it to her as an engagement ring. She wished me to share it with someone...special. I couldn't part with it—it didn't feel right—until now."

As if by magic, it slid easily onto my ring finger. My heart did that hard *thud* again and then skipped a beat. "It's...perfect." I glanced up into his eyes and the moonlight caught in them. Violet eyes—he'd inherited them from his mother. "Do you think she's right? The princess? She said violet eyes run in the Fae bloodline. Could your mother have been one?"

His grin was rakish. "I've wondered myself. She had

many unusual traits, but I honestly have no idea. I'm hoping you'll help me investigate this possibility when we have time."

The vampire loved a good mystery. One of the reasons he continued to work for SMG. When you'd lived for three hundred years, you'd been there, done that, and life could be rather boring, as he'd told me. Investigating crimes and other mysteries kept his intelligent mind stimulated. "I would love to."

"I wish to marry you. Properly." He paused, still toying with the ring now on my finger. The slight crease between his brows told me he was worried. Highly unusual. Even after his three centuries, and a previous marriage to boot, he could still be nervous. Who knew? "If you'll have me. I do not wish to pressure you."

"Didn't we just clear that up?"

The crease evaporated. "I need to hear you say 'yes'."

I threw my arms around him and the tears I'd been holding onto spilled over.

When the worst of my crying jag was finished and I'd soaked the shoulder of his expensive jacket, he drew back and fished out a pristine handkerchief. "It was not my intention to upset you."

I pointed at my wet cheeks, rubbing mascara off. "These are happy, dummy."

"Is that a 'yes,' then?" He scrutinized my face, his own vulnerable in a way I'd never seen. "I thought I might suggest we host the ceremony at the castle."

"*Are you kidding me?*" Now who was a princess? "A Christmas wedding in Romania? In a vampire's castle?" I squealed. It was so *not* me, yet I could barely contain myself. "Yes, *da*, for sure, abso-freakin-lutely."

"I shall fly in your family and friends who wish to attend."

"And Pennyworth, and Omwee, and Katarina, and Moss. Everyone, right?"

"You will be surrounded by those who love you and whom you love."

My heart was seriously going to melt.

"One warning."

"What?"

"Mixing vampires and humans does potentially pose problems."

I chuckled. "None of your nest will hurt my family or friends. They know better. Between the two of us, we'll keep everyone in line."

He smiled but looked doubtful. "The town is...not friendly to my kind. It is small and rather old-world."

"We'll stay in the castle."

He brightened. "It is secluded. High in the mountains. With the snowfall that time of year, it will be even more so."

I patted his chest. "See? It will be wonderful!"

"You are truly happy about it?"

"I'm over the moon."

The doubt left his face. He teased my jawline with his knuckles. "If you would prefer a diamond..." he started.

I cut him off with a kiss, the ruby a welcome weight on my finger. All my dreams were coming true. "All I need is you," I said against his lips.

He hugged me tight. "And I you. From now until forever."

Our promise to each other. The gem twinkled in the moonlight and I sighed. *From now until forever, yes indeed.*

CHLOE AND KILLION *are happy for now, but what will happen when they journey to his castle in Romania to wed? Find out in* **Grim Tidings**, *coming fall 2023!*

CAN'T WAIT for more of this pair? Don't miss the short story, **Grave Magic**, coming summer of 2023! This novella will be offered for free to my VIP newsletter subscribers before it's available for purchase at retailers, so be sure you're signed up http://eepurl.com/bP19Lr

DID you miss The Vampire's Kiss where Killion and Chloe bond? It's an exclusive in my direct buy store! **The Vampire's Kiss**

Paranormal Urban Fantasy:

The Accidental Reaper Series

Grim & Bare It

Killin' It (short story for newsletter subscribers only)

Reaper's Keepers

In too Reap

The Vampire's Kiss (an exclusive short story available ONLY on Misty's Store. *Intended for mature audiences 17+*)

Grave Girl (January 2023)

The Kali Sweet Series

Revenge Is Sweet, Kali Sweet Urban Fantasy Series, Book 1

Sweet Chaos, Kali Sweet Urban Fantasy Series, Book 2

Sweet Soldier, Kali Sweet Urban Fantasy Series, Book 3

Sweet Curse, Kali Sweet Urban Fantasy Series, Book 4

Paranormal Contemporary Romance:

Witches Anonymous Step 1

Jingle Hells, WA Step 2

Wicked Souls, WA Step 3

Dark Moon Lilith, Witches Anonymous Step 4

Dancing With the Devil, Witches Anonymous Step 5

Devil's Due, Witches Anonymous Step 6

Dirty Deeds, Witches Anonymous Step 7

Wicked Wedding, Witches Anonymous Step 8

Paranormal Romantic Suspense:

Soul Survivor, Moon Water Series, Book 1

Soul Protector, Moon Water Series, Book 2

Cozy Mysteries (writing as Nyx Halliwell):

Sister Witches Of Raven Falls Mystery Series

Sister Witches of Raven Falls Special Collection

Of Potions and Portents

Of Curses and Charms

Of Stars and Spells

Of Spirits and Superstition

Confessions of a Closet Medium Cozy Mystery Series

Confessions of a Closet Medium Special Collection

Pumpkins & Poltergeists

Magic & Mistletoe

Hearts & Haunts

Vows & Vengeance

Cupcakes & Corpses

Tea Leaves & Troubled Spirits

Sister Witches of Story Cove (Formerly Once Upon a Witch) Cozy Mystery Series

Cinder

Belle

Snow

Ruby

Zelle

MEET MISTY

USA TODAY Bestselling Author Misty Evans has published over eighty novels and writes romantic suspense, urban fantasy, and paranormal romance. Under her pen name, Nyx Halliwell, she writes cozy mysteries. Her nonfiction inspiration journals are also available in print from retailers.

When not reading or writing, she enjoys music, movies, and hanging out with her husband, twin sons, and three spoiled puppies. She's a crafter at heart and has far too many projects to finish.

Don't want to miss a single adventure? Visit www.mistyevansbooks.com to become a VIP and find out ALL the news!

Check out her humorous pen name Nyx Halliwell for magical mysteries https://www.nyxhalliwell.com .

Hello Beautiful Reader!

Thank you for reading this story! It is an honor and a privilege to write books for you. I'm an indie author and every fan is important to me. I pour my heart into each story and do my best to bring you an escape from the real world.

I hope you enjoyed this one, and if so, would you mind leaving a review at your favorite retailer? Or share your enjoyment of it with a friend or family member? I'd really appreciate it, and reviews help other readers find books they will love, too.

Readers are the key to my success - not a traditional publishing deal (had four), an agent (had two), or a publicity team (yep, you guessed it, had several of those as well.)

Those of you who read my books and love my characters and worlds, and who then tell others are like the best of friends. I adore you and will keep writing if you keep reading!

If you'd like to learn about my other books, sales, and special promotions, please sign up for my newsletter at **www.mistyevansbooks.com**. You'll get coupons to download starter packs for FREE, whether you love my romantic suspense or my paranormal. I also have a spy quiz, and a book list you can download and print.

Support me directly (no retailer taking their cut), grab special edition box sets, and get new releases before they are out at retailers by visiting my store **https://mistye vansbooks.com/shop**. I have sales and offer NEW RELEASES early! Check it out.

Last but not least, if you enjoy clean, cozy mysteries, visit my pen name **www.nyxhalliwell.com** to see those books.

Thank you and happy reading!
Misty

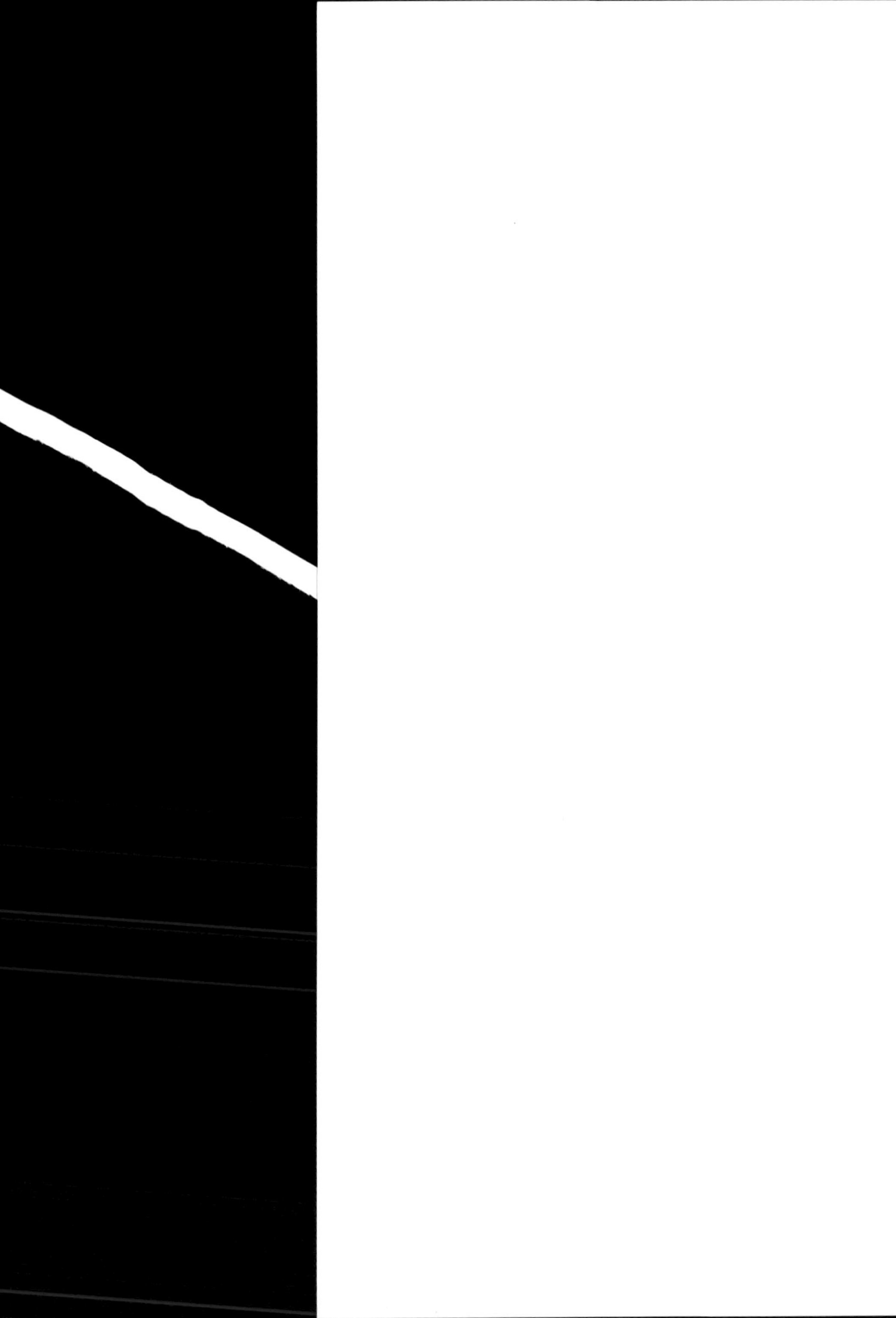